"You wanted me to come," he said, his gaze locking with hers.

A tiny nod, then the words, "I needed you to."

Needed. He hadn't needed a woman since he was twenty. He didn't *need* now. He could leave. Could walk out the door, get in his car and drive away as if nothing had ever happened. As if it might not kill him.

He didn't *need* to stay.

But he wanted to.

Another gust of wind rustled through the house, stirring his hair. She raised her hand as if to brush it back but hesitated, her fingers unsteady between them. He couldn't breathe, couldn't move, couldn't look at anything but her fingers, couldn't want anything but her fingers on him. Stroking him. Holding him. Arousing him…

And finally, finally, she touched him. Her fingertips brushed his hair, something his mother and grandmother had done dozens of times since he was a child, simple, innocent.

And so damn intimate that he hurt with it.

Dear Reader,

When Robbie Calloway first appeared in my head, I wasn't thinking about making him a hero. He was spoiled, arrogant, lazy and obnoxious—not exactly the commitment-worthy, true-love type. On the contrary, when Anamaria Duquesne came along, I knew she was heroine material. I just never intended for Robbie to be her perfect match. As so often happens when I write, the characters surprised me. They knew they were meant for each other even if I didn't.

But that's the cool thing about falling in love, isn't it? Two people can appear on the surface to have nothing in common, but deep down inside, they share the kind of connection that…well, that romance novels are made of. Anamaria calls it destiny. I call it happily ever after.

I hope *Scandal in Copper Lake* brings some sizzle to your February!

Marilyn

USA TODAY BESTSELLING AUTHOR

MARILYN PAPPANO

Scandal in Copper Lake

Silhouette

Romantic

SUSPENSE

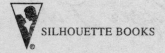

SILHOUETTE BOOKS

Recycling programs
for this product may
not exist in your area.

ISBN-13: 978-0-373-27617-2
ISBN-10:   0-373-27617-6

SCANDAL IN COPPER LAKE

Books by Marilyn Pappano

Silhouette Romantic Suspense

Within Reach #182
The Lights of Home #214
Guilt by Association #233
Cody Daniels' Return #258
Room at the Inn #268
Something of Heaven #294
Somebody's Baby #310
Not Without Honor #338
Safe Haven #363
A Dangerous Man #381
Probable Cause #405
Operation Homefront #424
Somebody's Lady #437
No Retreat #469
Memories of Laura #486
Sweet Annie's Pass #512
Finally a Father #542
*Michael's Gift #583
*Regarding Remy #609
*A Man Like Smith #626
Survive the Night #703
Discovered: Daddy #746
*Convincing Jamey #812
**The Taming of
  Reid Donovan* #824

*Knight Errant #836
The Overnight Alibi #848
Murphy's Law #901
**Cattleman's Promise #925
**The Horseman's Bride #957
**Rogue's Reform #1003
Who Do You Love? #1033
"A Little Bit Dangerous"
My Secret Valentine #1053
**The Sheriff's Surrender #1069
*The Princess and
  the Mercenary* #1130
**Lawman's Redemption #1159
**One True Thing #1280
**The Bluest Eyes in Texas #1391
Somebody's Hero #1427
More Than a Hero #1453
One Stormy Night #1471
Forbidden Stranger #1495
Intimate Enemy #1529
Scandal in Copper Lake #1547

*Southern Knights
**Heartbreak Canyon

MARILYN PAPPANO

has spent most of her life growing into the person she was meant to be, but isn't there yet. She's been blessed by family—her husband, their son, his lovely wife and a grandson who is almost certainly the most beautiful and talented baby in the world—and friends, along with a writing career that's made her one of the luckiest people around. Her passions, besides those already listed, include the pack of wild dogs who make their home in her house, fighting the good fight against the weeds that make up her yard, killing the creepy-crawlies that slither out of those weeds and, of course, anything having to do with books.

To Robert, my own connection, destiny and happily-ever-after. Here's to the next thirty years.

Chapter 1

Anamaria Duquesne slowed to a stop at the intersection and gazed up at the street sign. When Mama Odette had told her she would be living on Easy Street in Copper Lake, Georgia, she'd taken the words for symbolism. Mama Odette liked symbolism.

But her grandmother hadn't been striving for some deeper meaning. The street really was named Easy, though it was clearly a place where some hard living went on. For every streetlamp that glowed in the night, another two were burned out. The street was narrow and lacked shoulders but dipped into ditches that filled with water when it rained. Trees and bushes grew thick, and grass was sparse. The ten houses she passed before reaching the end of the street hadn't seen a new coat of paint in her lifetime. The cars were old, and a couple of scroungy-looking dogs stretched to the end of their chains to watch as she pulled into the last driveway.

She sat for a moment, studying the scene in the headlights'

beams. There was only one tree in the front, a magnificent live oak that shaded the entire front lawn. On the sides, the grass had long since surrendered to weeds that were thigh-high. The house was square, not large, but big enough for a mother and her daughter.

A screened porch stretched across the front; she knew from memory that the door opened into a central hall. On the left was the living room and, on the right, a bedroom. At the rear, there was a kitchen and another bedroom. A bathroom separated the two bedrooms.

This was the house where Anamaria had lived the first five years of her life. Just her and her mama, and a black puppy named Ebony. Ebony had made the move to Savannah with Anamaria. Her mama had not.

Despite the warm spring night, a chill crept across Anamaria's skin. She cut the engine and climbed out of the car, pausing to listen, smell, remember. She heard tree frogs, whip-poor-wills, a night train on the not-too-distant tracks. A faraway dog barking, an answering bark, a car. She smelled dampness from the nearby river, the lush new growth in the woods that backed the house, the faint scents of decay, despair…hopelessness.

And she remembered…very little. Climbing the live oak. Helping with her mother's flower garden. Playing with her mama as if they were both children.

Glory Duquesne had been little more than a child when she'd given birth to her first child at sixteen. This led to her dropping out of school, following the path with men and motherhood that Mama Odette had taken, and every other Duquesne woman before them. She had been beautiful—not just a daughter's memory but verified by photographs—with café-au-lait skin, coarse black hair, eyes as brown as the earth and a smile that could stop a man in his tracks.

It's a curse, Mama Odette said. *Duquesne women love well and long and unwisely, and we never marry. But we make beautiful daughters.* It was hard to tell with her whether *It's a curse* meant an actual curse. Mama Odette believed in the old ways, in evil and curses and The Sight and atonement. She'd supported first her own babies, then her grandbaby, by telling fortunes, offering healing and charms and advice.

Taking two suitcases from the trunk, Anamaria made her way across the yard and climbed creaky steps to the porch. There were tears in the screens, along with enough rust to obscure the view. She crossed to the door, fumbled with the lock, then stepped inside and flipped the light switch. She'd called ahead to the power company, so light illuminated the hallway.

For a time she stood just inside the door, anticipation—fear?—tightening her lungs. Then she drew a breath. She'd expected *something.* Some flood of memories. Some sense of Mama. Some feeling of horror. But nothing came. The few memories she'd already examined were it.

Thanks to the cleaning service she'd hired, the house smelled of furniture polish and wood soap. Twenty-three years of abandonment had been scrubbed away, leaving the rooms spotless but shabby. The wallpaper was faded, the furniture outdated, the linoleum worn. The metal kitchen cabinets were fifty years or older, but the refrigerator and stove were in working order. There was no dishwasher and no microwave, but she didn't mind.

Walking along the hall, she wished for a memory, a whisper, a ghost. But talking to the dead was Mama Odette's strength. Those who'd passed ignored Anamaria as thoroughly as the living ignored them. They dismissed her, finding her unworthy of their endless supply of time.

She stopped in the doorway of her old room but didn't

venture inside. There was one other memory tied to this small, dark, unwelcoming room, of her five-year-old self sobbing in bed, terrified by the first vision she'd ever seen. If she stepped across the threshold, she might hear the faint echoes, feel the faint shudders, hear her own hysterical words. *She's in the water. Mama's in the water.*

Maybe she'd cross the threshold sometime. But not tonight.

She backtracked the few feet to the bathroom: sink, toilet, tub, leaky shower. The last room was Mama's bedroom. Three windows each on the outside walls. Iron bed frame, walnut veneer dresser, oak veneer night table. Faded paint. Empty closet.

After Mama Odette had moved Anamaria to her house in Savannah, Auntie Lueena and her daughters had packed up only the personal belongings from this house—the clothing, the toys, the mementos. The furniture, lacking value, had stayed. Lueena had broached the subject of selling the place, but Mama Odette had refused. It wasn't theirs to sell; it belonged to Anamaria.

She smiled thinly. A shabby old house on Easy Street. A few good memories, one truly horrific one. Not much of a legacy for Glory.

No, she corrected herself as she lifted one suitcase onto the dresser top and opened it. Glory's legacy was her children: Lillie, who'd gone to live with her father's people when she was a baby. Jass, who'd done the same three years later. Anamaria, whose father remained a mystery.

And the newborn infant who'd died when her mother had.

She unpacked everything she'd brought—clothing, toiletries, dishes, groceries—then made the bed, changed into a nightgown and sat cross-legged on the bed with an ancient wooden chest in front of her.

The box was built of tropical wood, heavily carved with

symbols and words in another language. Duquesne women loved unhampered by taboos. Race had never mattered to them; the blood and beliefs of Anamaria's male ancestors ran far and wide.

Love was all that mattered to Duquesne women. Hot, passionate, greedy, breath-stealing love.

Glory had excelled at that kind of love. Lillie's father had been the first true love of her life, followed by Jass's father. *Did Mama love my daddy?* Anamaria had once asked, and Mama Odette had assured her she did. *But she didn't even know who he was,* Anamaria had protested.

But she loved him, chile. Your mama loved every man in her life just like he was the onliest one.

Nerves dancing on edge, Anamaria rubbed her fingers over the carved lid. Family history said the chest had been a wedding gift to Lucia Duquesne, filled with gems and gold coins by her lover. Come the wedding day, though, Lucia had disappeared, the chest with her. Now it held part of Anamaria's family history. Mementos of the years she'd lived in this house with Mama. Memories she couldn't retrieve from their hiding places in her head.

She opened the filigreed gold latch, hesitated, then folded it back into place. She would delve into the chest's mysteries, but not tonight. She was too unsettled. She needed to locate her center of peace before she lifted the lid on her greatest love, her greatest loss.

Rising, she placed the chest in the darkest corner of the closet. For good measure, she pulled an empty suitcase over to block it from sight, then returned to the bed.

It was early for sleep, but she'd begun a long journey that day, longer than the one hundred and twenty-five miles between Savannah and Copper Lake suggested. She had an even longer road ahead of her.

She was going to find out everything she could about her mother's life in this town.

And her death.

Office hours at Robbie Calloway's law practice were nine to five for his secretary, one to five for his paralegal and pretty much whenever he couldn't avoid showing up for him. On the second Tuesday in April, that was eleven o'clock, and then only because he had a last-minute appointment.

Ursula Benton, his second cousin's mother-in-law, looked up when he walked in at five till. With glasses perched on the end of her nose and her fingertips on the computer keyboard, it appeared she was hard at work. But Robbie knew it was more likely that she was chatting online about her passion in life, cross-stitching, than doing anything work-related.

"He's in your office," she said. "Here are your messages."

He accepted a handful of yellow slips. Except for a call from his mother, Sara, the rest were from attorneys or clients. He tried to keep his client load to the bare minimum needed to justify an office and two employees. Law wasn't a career for him; it was an interesting diversion. Thanks to a family who'd always had good fortune, he didn't need the income. And unlike his brothers, Rick, Mitch and Russ, he wasn't all that enamored with real work.

However, Harrison Kennedy, who was waiting in the office, did require real work of Robbie from time to time. After the Calloways, the Kennedys were the wealthiest and most influential family in this part of Georgia. Harrison had been friends with Robbie's father, Gerald, until his death, and his wife, Lydia, remained Sara's closest friend.

Harrison was standing at the window, gazing out over the Gullah River, a glass of whiskey in hand. Robbie glanced at the brownish liquid, his mouth watering, before helping himself to a bottle of water and going to stand at the opposite end of the window.

"A good day to be out there with a fishing pole and a cooler of beer." Harrison stared out the window a moment longer before turning to face him. "I didn't get you out of bed too early, did I?"

Robbie ignored the sarcasm. "Nah, I'm always up in time for lunch."

Harrison believed in long hours and hard work. It was how he made his fortune, he often declared. Truth was, he'd inherited his fortune, just like Gerald, and he'd added to it by marrying into an even bigger one. Granted, he'd probably doubled it since then, but making more money wasn't so hard when he already had plenty.

"What can I do for you?" Robbie asked.

Harrison picked up a folder from the credenza, removed a page and slapped it down between them. "I want to know everything you can find out about her."

It wasn't a great photo, taken by the security camera at the gate to the Kennedy property and printed on plain white paper, but it was enough to make any red-blooded man take a second look. The woman was beautiful, exotic. Eyes the color of cocoa; skin the color of cocoa in milk; lush lips; a long, lovely throat; sleek black hair. She wore an orange top, chunky earrings and an air of self-assurance.

Underneath the photo, someone had scrawled a few bits of information: *Anamaria Duquesne. Glory Duquesne.* There was a date and a time—yesterday afternoon—and a description of a car, along with the tag number.

"Who is she?"

Harrison pointed at the page. "Anamaria Duquesne. Glory Duquesne's daughter."

There was something about the way his eyes were moving,

the way he suddenly shifted his weight from one foot to the other. He thrust his hands into his pants pockets, a habit he deplored—*Ruins the line of a good suit*—then pulled them out again.

Robbie waited. He was very good at doing nothing while seconds ticked past.

Harrison tugged at his tie, then exhaled. "You know Liddy is a smart woman. A sensible one, most of the time."

Robbie nodded.

Harrison tugged at his tie again. "She has a thing for…an interest in…you know. Weird stuff. Psychics. Talking to the dead. Fortune-telling."

Though he hid it, Robbie couldn't have been more surprised if he'd said pornography or drugs. Lydia wasn't just sensible; she was about as no-nonsense as they came. She had an abiding faith in God, country and family, right and wrong, good and evil, logic and bunk. She didn't trifle with anything the least bit, well, trifling. And she was into what Robbie's last ex fondly called "woo-woo"?

"It started when the baby died," Harrison went on. "She was so down. Everything had gone so well—the pregnancy, the labor, the delivery. And three hours later… She blamed herself. She didn't cry. She didn't let go. She just sort of disappeared inside herself. Then she started seeing that woman—Glory Duquesne.

"Your uncle Cyrus checked her out for me at the time. She'd never been married. She had three children by three men. She didn't have custody of the older two girls, just that one." Harrison gestured toward the photo. "She lived on the wrong side of town and made a living taking money from people who were vulnerable. She was a con artist, preying on the weak, and after the baby died, God, was Liddy weak."

Lydia and Harrison had lost their only child over twenty years ago, which would explain why Robbie had never heard of the Duquesnes. A lot of people came and went in twenty years, and in the Copper Lake of that era, they kept to their proper places while they were there. It was doubtful that he'd ever crossed paths with either Glory Duquesne or her daughter.

Harrison's hand shook as he drained the whiskey, then set the glass down with a thud. "I knew the woman was a phony, but she wasn't charging any more than the doctor whose best idea was to medicate Liddy into a fog. And she seemed to help Liddy find some peace, so I was more than happy to pay for their once-a-week sessions. And then, about a year after Liddy started seeing her, the woman…"

His jaw tightened, and he bit out the last words. "She died."

"How?" Robbie asked, gazing again at the photograph. Anamaria Duquesne couldn't have been more than six, maybe seven years old at the time, a little older than he'd been when his father died. He'd hardly known his old man, though, and Sara had made sure he'd never missed him. Had there been a father to take in Anamaria? Family somewhere who wanted her?

"Accident, the police said. She went for a walk along the river at night, fell and hit her head. They found her body, snagged on some branches, half in the water." Harrison reached for the glass again and looked surprised that it was empty. His tone turned grimmer. "She was nine months pregnant. Coroner said the fall caused her to go into labor and that the baby… His best guess was that the baby was washed away by the river. It was never found."

"God." No wonder Robbie hadn't heard the story before. He'd been a typical kid, outside running wild most of the time, and his only use for the Copper Lake *Clarion* or a news broadcast had been the scores for his favorite teams. A pregnant mother dying alone in the night, with her newborn baby swept away to drown in the river, was definitely something his mother wouldn't have discussed in front of him.

But all that was history. "What's happening now?"

"Liddy got a call yesterday from the girl. Said she was in town and had a message for Liddy and could she come over to deliver it. It was some mumbo jumbo—something about a white-haired man and flowers."

"Did she ask for money?"

"No. And Liddy didn't offer her any." Harrison's mouth took on a pinched look. "That time. But she's got an appointment to see her tomorrow morning. The girl's promised another message."

Like mother, like daughter. Anamaria had been just a child when her mother died. Had she observed that much of Glory's scams in that short time, or had someone else taken over her education after Glory's death?

Robbie moved to sit on the edge of his desk. "I can recommend a good private investigator."

"What can a private investigator do that you can't?"

Nothing, as far as gathering information went. Robbie had access to the same databases, and while he wasn't the most Internet-savvy person around, his paralegal was. And he had an in that most PIs didn't: Tommy Maricci, his best bud since they'd given each other black eyes on the first day of kindergarten, was a detective with the Copper Lake Police Department. Granted, Tommy's help would be bending the law more than a little, but it was for a good cause.

"I've never had any experience at surveilling or following anyone. I'm not exactly covert when I go out."

"I don't want you to be subtle," Harrison said. "I want her to know she's being watched. I want her to understand that if she says one thing to upset Liddy, she'll pay dearly. Find out who she is, what she's up to, why she's here…and then put the fear of God into her so that she goes away."

Robbie smiled thinly. He could do that. He might be only

a part-time lawyer, but he gave his all to every case. There was nothing sweeter than that moment when he knew he'd prevailed, except the moment when his opponent knew it, too.

"Can I talk to Lydia?"

Harrison didn't hesitate. "No."

"But—"

"No. Leave her out of this."

That might be hard to do, considering that without Lydia, there was no *this*. But Robbie nodded in agreement. "I'll let you know what I find out."

Harrison nodded, slapped him on the back affectionately then left the office.

Robbie sat down at his desk, sliding the computer keyboard closer, then braced the phone between his ear and shoulder while he signed online.

A few hours later, he leaned back in the chair and watched a boat pass on the river. It hadn't taken long in this computer-centric age to learn pretty much all there was to know about Anamaria Duquesne. She was twenty-eight years old. Lived on Queen Street in Savannah. Had been raised by her grandmother, Odette Duquesne, after her mother's death. Worked part-time at her aunt Lueena Duquesne's restaurant a few blocks from her home. Also worked part-time telling fortunes.

She had two credit cards, paid in full every month, and had earned enough points to buy herself a round-trip flight to anywhere in the world. She was down to the last four payments on her car. She'd taken a few classes at the local community college—nothing toward a degree, just Spanish, art, cooking. She'd been arrested a few times for her phony-seer act, but the charges had been dropped. She'd never been sued, gotten a traffic ticket or applied for a passport. She had never been married, had no children, and her father was listed on her birth certificate as Unknown.

He knew a lot, but he'd learned nothing, really. The important questions—why she'd come to Copper Lake, what she wanted with Liddy Kennedy—could be answered only by her.

He had her phone number, but he didn't bother calling. He also had her local address. The only property she owned besides her car was a sixty-five-year-old house at the end of Easy Street.

He said goodbye to Ursula, then took the stairs to the garage below. He'd bought the building in part for its location on River Road—Copper Lake's main drag—and in part for its view of the Gullah River, but mostly for the private garage on the ground level. He'd put too damn many hours and too damn much money into restoring his '57 Vette to mint condition to park it just anywhere. The engine gave a finely tuned roar as he backed out of the space, then turned onto River Road.

Just north of downtown was a neighborhood of pricey old homes, each sitting on an acre or two of stately trees and manicured lawn. Holigan Creek, curving west to empty into the river, formed the boundary between that neighborhood, where Russ's wife, Jamie, had once lived, and the poor white neighborhood where Rick's wife, Amanda, had grown up. The lots were smaller there, the houses more cramped, the yards shaggier. A marshy patch separated that area from the poor black neighborhood, which had only one way in or out. Tillman Avenue led off to a half-dozen other streets, each with its own collection of sorry, run-down houses.

The Duquesne house was the last one in the neighborhood. Easy Street dead-ended at its driveway, and fifty yards separated it from the homes on either side. There was no paint on the weathered siding, and the roof showed spots where shingles had blown away, but other than that, there was a sturdiness about the house.

He parked behind Anamaria Duquesne's two-door sedan

and got out to the accompaniment of dogs barking. There was no sign of anyone around, but he couldn't shake the feeling that he was being watched, both from the houses behind him and from the one ahead.

He was proven right about the latter when he opened the screen door at the top of the steps. Anamaria sat in an old wooden rocker, one leg propped over the chair arm, the other foot planted on the floor. She wore a sleeveless dark orange blouse and a long full skirt in eye-popping orange, red and yellow print. The extra fabric was tucked between her legs, giving some semblance of modesty, and it rustled as she kept the chair in motion with the foot on the floor.

Her hair was up that afternoon, baring that long, lovely neck, and her lids were heavy, as if the heat of the day and the peace of the porch had lulled her someplace else. But that, Robbie thought, was an act. She was as aware of him as he was of her.

After a moment, the rocking stopped and she let her leg slide down. Both feet were bare except for a coat of deep red polish on the toenails. No toe ring. No bracelet circling her delicate ankle.

"Robbie Calloway," she said at last.

"How did you know? Oh, my God, you must be psychic," he said drily. Crossing the porch, he sat in another rocker that creaked with each backstroke.

She smiled at his response. "It's been a long time since you've gone anywhere in Copper Lake without being recognized. After all, you're not just a Calloway. You're one of *the* Calloways. You, your brothers, your mother—you're considered the best of the best."

"And you know this…?"

"I'm psychic, remember? And I read the paper. I talk to people." She leaned forward and extended her right hand. "I'm—"

"Anamaria Duquesne. You scam people for a living." He took her hand as he spoke and felt her muscles tighten at his remark. She didn't try to pull away, though, even if he was holding on far too long for a handshake. Her skin was soft and warm, and it made him wonder if she felt like that all over. She was gorgeous with her clothes on. He could only imagine how stunning she would be with them off.

When he let go of her hand, she sat back and crossed one leg over the other. "You know what they call ten lawyers at the bottom of the sea? A good start. You have some nerve, criticizing what I do for a living." Her voice was soft, fluid, the accent pure coastal Georgia. It was a voice that could quiet a cranky child, soothe a troubled soul or arouse a man until he hurt. If she ever took her clairvoyant nonsense to the radio, every man within listening range, believer or not, would tune in just to hear that voice.

"I understand you used to live here," he said.

"A long time ago."

"Why are you here now?"

She smiled faintly. "Because I used to live here. Why are you here?" Before he could answer, she went on. "Let me guess. Harrison Kennedy asked you to check me out."

"Do you blame him?"

Her brows arched as she shrugged. "I've done nothing wrong."

"You have an arrest record."

Another shrug. "You would have one, too, if you weren't a Calloway, and for more serious charges than my own."

Robbie couldn't argue the fact with her. He and his brothers had gotten into a lot of trouble when they were kids. There was no doubt that the family name, as well as Granddad, had kept them out of jail on more than one occasion.

"What do you call what you do?" he continued.

"A gift. Sometimes, not so much."

He gestured. "Are you a psychic? Seer? Reader? Palmist? Do you have a sign outside your house in Savannah that says Sister Anamaria Sees All, with an evil eye and a palm, a moon and some stars?"

"I'm an advisor. No signs."

"Then how do your customers find you?"

"Everyone in Savannah knows where to find Mama Odette's girl." Uncrossing her legs, she stood gracefully. Her skirt flowed around her in psychedelic ripples. "Would you like a glass of fresh-squeezed lemonade? I use Auntie Lueena's recipe. I'm sure you know who she is."

"Sure. Why not?"

She went to the door, opened it, then turned back to give him a devilish smile. "And I promise, Robbie Calloway, I won't doctor it with anything. Healing or otherwise."

It took only a moment to fill two glasses with ice, another to remove the pitcher from the refrigerator. Balancing it all, she carried it through the quiet house and onto the porch. The pitcher was already sweating when she set it on a small table, then filled the glasses.

"What is it exactly that Mr. Kennedy wants to know about me?" She handed one glass to Robbie, careful not to touch him, then sat down again in Mama's rocker, cradling her own glass between her palms.

"Who you are. Why you're here. What you're up to."

"You know who I am. Do I need an explanation for coming to stay at a house I've owned for twenty-three years? As for what I'm up to…I'm resting. Taking a break from my regular life. Retreating." After a long drink of lemonade, she went on. "I suspect Mr. Kennedy's primary interest is what I want with Miss Lydia."

"What *do* you want with Miss Lydia?"

"For me, nothing. My mother had a message for her that I agreed to pass on."

Skepticism crossed Robbie's face. "You talk to your dead mother?"

Ignoring the sting of pain deep inside, Anamaria shook her head. "I don't have that ability. She speaks to my grandmother." As a small child, Anamaria would have been afraid to suddenly hear Mama's voice again. As a teenager, she would have given a lot to hear her say one more time, *Everything's gonna be all right, baby doll.* As an adult, she felt snubbed. She hadn't asked for any sort of abilities, but if she had to have something, why couldn't it have been the one gift that would allow her to connect with the mother she missed so desperately?

"What are your abilities?"

She smiled the aloof, mysterious sort of smile that customers always responded to. "I can read your palm, your tea leaves or your cards. I can look into your future and tell you something so vague it could be taken a dozen ways. I can gaze into the crystal ball or throw the bones or study your astral charts and give you information so startlingly imprecise that it could apply to anything or nothing at all."

"So you're a total fraud." He grinned. He was handsome enough when his mouth was set in a grim line, but when he grinned... That flash of blinding-white teeth made his dark hair darker, his blue eyes bluer, his bronzed skin damn near lustrous.

A warning sounded distantly in her mind. Men and love were the downfall of the Duquesne women, together more dangerous than anything else they might face. So far, she had managed to avoid feeling passionately about anyone, but she was always on watch, always drawing away.

But if any man was safe for her, it was this one. Robbie

Calloway was the most elite of an elite group. He was white, very socially aware, raised with two hundred years of teaching that the races didn't mingle. His family, his church, his country club, his office, his circle of friends—all white. He'd dated enough women to populate a sorority house or two— all white. He wasn't a threat to Anamaria.

Though he might make her a threat to herself.

"Did you take time from your busy workday just to check me out?"

His smile was wry. "Yeah, I lead a busy life. Twenty hours a week in the office is about ten too many for my tastes."

"I thought you were a successful lawyer." She hadn't lied about reading the newspaper; reading back issues of the *Clarion* had been one of the first things she'd done once she'd decided to make this journey. His name appeared on a regular basis, as much for professional activities as for social ones.

"I am successful. I just don't see the point of expending too much time or energy at it."

"It's not your passion?"

He drained his lemonade, then set the glass next to the pitcher. She asked with a gesture if he'd like more; he shook his head. "I feel passionate about some of my cases, but the job itself? No. Is scamming—sorry, I mean advising—people your passion?"

"One of them." She loved her work, her family, her job at Auntie Lueena's diner. The only thing that could make her life better was having her mother and baby sister in it.

"What are the others?"

"That's an impertinent question to ask someone you've just met."

Robbie shrugged, his deep-green shirt rippling over nice muscles. "What was the message for Lydia Kennedy?"

The change of subject caught Anamaria off guard, though she hid it. "That's Miss Lydia's business. It's not my place to share."

"If I ask her, she'll tell me."

"So ask her."

He studied her a moment, then slowly smiled. "I'll do that."

She doubted Lydia would have any qualms about sharing. The message had been innocent enough: good wishes from a white-haired man who loved to garden, along with a reminder to look out for his prized irises. It really had come from Glory, through Mama Odette, though no doubt Robbie was skeptical. He was a lawyer who believed in evidence, hard facts. Anamaria was a dreamer who took many things on faith. His feet were firmly planted in his reality; she was adrift in her own.

"How long will you be staying in Copper Lake?"

"I don't know. Maybe long enough for Mr. Kennedy to finance another toy for you." She waved one hand languidly in the direction of the Corvette. Automobiles were transportation to her, nothing more. Mama Odette had never owned a car or learned to drive. Even now, closing in on seventy, she preferred her own two feet for getting around. That was why the good Lord gave them to her, wasn't it?

Anamaria prayed the good Lord would let her grandmother continue getting around. She was having a hard time recovering from this last stint in the hospital. Her heart was weak, the cardiologist said. Maybe not so much, Mama Odette had declared with a wink. *There's still livin' left to do. Fortunes to tell, places to go, people to meet.*

Robbie looked offended at her description of his car. "That's the sweetest car this side of Atlanta. She has 327 cubes at 365 horsepower and tops out at 140 miles per hour."

The words meant nothing to her. Duquesne women weren't mechanically inclined, but they had a knack for finding men who were. "A high-performance toy. It won't take you anywhere my Honda won't go."

"No, but I'll get there in style," he said with a grin as he rose from the rocker. It creaked in protest a few times—at the movement? Or his leaving?

Anamaria stood, as well, and walked to the screen door with him. She was tall, five-ten in her bare feet, but he stood a few inches taller. He moved with the ease of someone who'd always known his place in the world. He did wondrous things for khakis and a polo shirt, and he smelled rich and sexy and very, very classy. He was most definitely what Auntie Lueena would call a fine catch—with four daughters, Lueena was ever hopeful that one would break the curse and marry—and yet he remained single.

It wasn't Anamaria's place to wonder why.

"Thank you for the lemonade and your time," he said as he passed through the doorway. On the second step he turned back, the charming smile still in place but absent from his eyes. "Watch your step with Lydia. She's like family to me, and you don't want to go messing with my family."

Anamaria leaned against the doorjamb, one arm out-stretched to hold the screen door open. "You don't want to go messing with Miss Lydia, either. She knows what she wants and how to get it."

He raised one hand as if to touch the strand of hair that had fallen loose from its clasp and now brushed her shoulder, then, only inches away, lowered it again. "You know what you want, too, don't you? And you know how to get it. Luckily, I know how to stop you."

With those words, he took the remaining steps two at a time, strode across the dirt and got behind the wheel of his expensive little car. She watched him back out in a tight turn, then accelerate down Easy Street before she closed the door and returned to the rocker.

Robbie Calloway didn't have a clue what she wanted. Like most skeptics, his distrust of her abilities also meant a distrust of her. She was a fraud in his eyes, not just as an advisor but as a person.

Her business was her business. What she'd said to Lydia, why she'd come to Copper Lake, everything she did…in the end, she bore sole responsibility for her actions, and she carried no regrets.

When she returned to Savannah, she would still have no regrets.

Especially not one named Robbie.

Chapter 2

Much of Copper Lake's downtown area showed its two-hundred-year-old roots: red bricks softened to a rosy hue, dimpled glass, wood glowing with a well-deserved patina. At the heart was the square, manicured grass bordered with flowers, war monuments and walkways leading to and from the bandstand that anchored the park.

Everywhere Anamaria looked, she saw beauty, prosperity…and the Calloway name—law offices, a construction company, doctors' and dentists' offices, investment and accounting firms, retail shops. Robbie Calloway's office was on River Road, the building only a few years old but built to blend in with its vintage neighbors.

Nice space for a man who thought ten hours a week in the office just fine. She worked sixty hours a week or more and would never own a place like that or a car like his. But she knew all too well that money didn't buy happiness and neither did things. People were the only thing that mattered, and all the money in the world couldn't buy the good ones.

Then she thought of the Civil War monument she'd just passed and amended that thought: *not anymore*. Such places as the Calloway Plantation and Twin Oaks, Lydia Kennedy's home, had undoubtedly relied on slave labor to do all the jobs that kept the families clothed, fed and wealthy. Slaves such as Ophelia, Harriett, Gussie and Florence Duquesne, their children and their grandchildren.

Turning onto Carolina Avenue, she drove east. A few miles past the town limits sign was Twin Oaks, but she was meeting Lydia in town today. The older woman had suggested they meet at River's Edge, the centerpiece of downtown. The Greek Revival mansion had undergone an extensive restoration and had been transformed into a beautiful white gem in the midst of an emerald-green lawn, all of it surrounded by a black wrought-iron fence. It was open to the public for tours, parties and weddings, Lydia had told her, but not on Wednesdays. They would have the place to themselves.

But with time to spare, Anamaria bypassed the street that would take her back to River's Edge. She drove aimlessly, past parks and schools and stores—not the pricey ones downtown but the cheaper, shabbier ones on the outskirts. She located the church she and Glory had attended—a small structure that looked every one of its one hundred forty years in spite of its fresh coat of white paint. She tried to remember using swings on this playground, getting enrolled for kindergarten at that school, shopping for groceries at this market, dressing up in her Sunday best and skipping into the church.

But nothing came. Her five years in Copper Lake had been diminished to a handful of memories.

The last place she searched out was Gullah Park. It was a long, narrow section of land nestled alongside the river just north of downtown. There was a parking lot, a small playground, a handful of concrete picnic tables and a paved trail that followed the riverbank out of sight.

She stopped at the entrance to the lot, her hands clammy, her fingers clenching the steering wheel. This was where her mother's car had been found that morning, parked all the way at the end. She'd come there to walk, the police had told Mama Odette.

Why? Mama Odette wanted to know. It was silly to get into a car and drive someplace just so you could walk. Not that Glory was above being silly from time to time—her silliness was one of the things Anamaria had loved best about her— but it struck her mother as strange even for her.

Mama Odette wanted to know everything. As she faced the last days of her life, she'd developed a burning need to know about the last days of Glory's life. The all-too-short time of the baby's life.

The blare of a horn behind her jerked Anamaria's gaze to the rearview mirror, where a man waited impatiently for her to move. As she drove on, he turned into the parking lot. She would come back here, get out and walk that trail. Sometimes she had visions, sometimes there were just feelings and sometimes she drew a blank. She hoped she would learn something. She didn't want to let Mama Odette down.

Back at the square, she found a parking space on the north side of River's Edge and entered the property through a side gate. Wide steps led to a broad gallery, its floor herringboned-brick, its ceiling painted sky blue. Sturdy wicker chairs, iron benches and wooden rockers were spaced along the porch, with pots of bright geraniums nestled at the base of each massive column.

When she turned the corner at the front of the house, Lydia was standing near the door, gazing at her watch. She looked up at the sound of Anamaria's footsteps and a welcoming smile crossed her face. "I couldn't remember whether we'd settled on ten or ten-thirty or if I'd told you the front gate would be locked, but here you are, straight-up ten o'clock. Come on in."

Like Anamaria's own house, the doorway opened into a hallway that ran front to back, with rooms opening off each side. Unlike her house, this hallway was fifteen feet wide and provided space for an elaborate staircase that would have done Rhett Butler and Scarlett O'Hara proud. The walls were painted deep red and were a backdrop to forbidding portraits and landscapes in heavy, aged oils.

"Our ancestors were a dour lot, weren't they?" Lydia remarked as she led the way down the hall.

"Some of them had a right to be." But not these stern men and women whose narrow gazes followed them. They'd had wealth, influence and people to provide their every need. Ophelia, Harriet, Gussie and Florence had had nothing but their family, their gifts and their love of life—not even their freedom—but in her heart Anamaria knew they'd been the happier of the two groups.

The door at the end of the hall led into a thoroughly modern kitchen with stainless-steel countertops, restaurant-grade appliances and, tucked away near a window, the cozy nook with padded benches that was their destination. A notebook lay open on the table, with snapshots of flowers scattered about. A cup of tea sat on one side; an empty cup waited on the other.

"I stopped at Ellie's Deli on the way and picked up some sweets," Lydia said, moving the box from the nearest counter to the tabletop. Inside were a dozen miniatures—tiny croissants, sticky buns no bigger than a golf ball, petit fours and pecan tartlets.

After they'd each chosen a pastry, Lydia sat back, her gaze settling on Anamaria's face. "You don't speak with those who have passed, do you?"

"No. That's my grandmother's gift."

"And when she received that message from Mr. John— that's what we all called Grandfather—you came all this way to deliver it?"

"I was planning the trip anyway. I imagine that's why Mr. John chose to speak to Mama Odette." If he hadn't, she would have used the straightforward approach and simply asked to meet with Lydia. But the dead didn't miss any opportunities, lucky for her.

Lydia gathered the photographs into a neat stack, then set them and the notebook aside. "I'm reworking some of the gardens. Those are notes and pictures from last summer. Harrison says I have fertilizer running through my veins—a gift from Mr. John. I prefer flowers over just about anything."

But not children…or grandchildren. Anamaria could practically see the longing, dulled now after years of childlessness but still there. Still clinging to her like a distant hope, nearly forgotten.

"Do you volunteer here?" Anamaria asked as she filled her cup from the china teapot, then sniffed the tendrils of steam that drifted up. Chamomile and lavender—Mama Odette's favorite blend.

"You could say that. I own River's Edge—or, rather, it owns me. It belonged to the Calloways for generations, then passed into, then out of, my family. When it became available again a few years ago, I bought it, hired out the renovation and have been working on the landscaping myself."

Lydia refilled her own cup, then breathed deeply of the aroma as Anamaria had done. "Your mother prescribed this for me. At first, she brought it to me in little paper bags, then she showed me how to mix it myself. I have a cup or two every day, and I always think of her."

Even Anamaria couldn't make that claim. Days went by when she couldn't honestly say she'd thought of her mother even once. She'd loved Glory, but she'd done virtually all of her growing up without her. All of the usual significant mother/daughter moments in her life involved Mama Odette or Auntie Lueena.

"I was so stunned when I heard what happened," Lydia went on, gazing into her cup as if she might read her fortune there. "All I could think was that poor child. She'd done nothing to deserve that. So young, so innocent."

For a moment, Anamaria thought *the poor child* meant Glory. She'd been only twenty-seven when she died, and she possessed a childlike enthusiasm and wonder for all that life had to offer. But innocent? Mama Odette claimed she was born knowing more than most women learned by the time they were thirty.

"Did you find another advisor?"

Lydia shook her head. "I was better. Your mother helped me more than I can say. And then…" She shook her head again, then, with a deep breath, changed the subject. "I should warn you that my husband isn't too happy that I'm meeting with you. He might do something foolishly overprotective."

"Such as instruct his lawyer to investigate me?" Anamaria asked with a wry smile.

"Oh, Lord. He did the same thing with your mother— asked his lawyer to look into her background. Then it was Cyrus Calloway, my brother-in-law and Robbie's uncle. We're practically family, the Kennedys and the Calloways."

"That's what Robbie said."

"So you've met him. Don't let him charm your socks off."

"I'm immune to charm."

Lydia wagged one finger in her direction. "Only because the right man hasn't tried. If I was thirty years younger, I'd take any one of Sara and Gerald's boys. Though the older three have wives now who would snatch me bald if I even got too close."

It was easy to see Robbie Calloway charming the socks—and everything else—off most women, but not her. He distrusted her. She had priorities. He thought she was a threat to Lydia. She was very good at guarding her heart. Someday she would experience that hot, passionate, greedy love—all Duquesne women did—but not now. Not here. Most definitely not with him.

"Why were you planning this trip?"

Another quick subject change, but Anamaria wasn't flustered. She'd known the question would come up, and she'd chosen the simplest, truthful answer. "Curiosity. I'm a year older now than my mother was when she died. I want to see where she lived, to talk to people who knew her. Mama Odette and Auntie Lueena have told me a lot, but I want to hear what other people know that they don't. I want to *know* her."

Lydia nodded sympathetically. "It must have been hard for your grandmother, losing both her daughter and her grandbaby at the same time."

"It broke her heart."

"And yours."

Anamaria nodded. She might not remember much of life with Glory, but she knew it must have been good, because living without her had been hard, even surrounded by family who loved her.

"You were a pretty little girl," Lydia went on. "I didn't see you often. Glory usually left you with a neighbor when she came to my house. But a few times, she brought you with her and you played in the garden while we talked. You wore frilly little dresses, and your hair was tied back with a bow. You'd say *yes, ma'am* and *thank you* and *please* just as solemn as could be. I told Glory she was blessed to have such a lovely daughter. And then she got blessed again."

A lot of people hadn't seen blessings anywhere around Glory. Instead, they'd seen a stereotype: an uneducated black woman, illegitimate children, no legitimate means of support. But Glory had fit nobody's stereotype.

"You loved the flowers in my garden, especially the lilies. You have a sister named Lillie, don't you?"

"I do. And another named Jass." Lillie was five years older and lived in South Carolina. Jass was two years older and living in Texas. They didn't miss Glory the way Anamaria did, but they'd never known her the way Anamaria had. They'd been raised by their fathers, by paternal grandmothers and aunts and stepmothers.

"And the baby would have been Charlotte."

Anamaria looked up, surprised. "Charlotte?"

"Surely you knew that. Glory decided on it about a month before she passed."

Another of those details that she'd shut out after the shock of seeing her mother dead. She tried the name in her mind: Charlotte Duquesne. *My sister, Charlotte.* Not just *the baby,* so generic and impersonal, but Charlotte, with café-au-lait skin, chocolate-colored eyes, wispy black hair and tiny features with the exotic stamp of all her mixed heritages. Having a name made her more real and made her absence sharper, more intense.

"So…" Lydia gazed across the table at her. "Glory used to say that you would follow in her footsteps. She said when you were three, you'd tell her someone was at the door a minute or two before they even stepped onto the porch. She said when you were four, all she had to do was *think* about fixing meat loaf for dinner, and you'd tell her no in no uncertain terms."

Anamaria smiled. To this day she couldn't stomach meat loaf. It was the Thursday special at Auntie Lueena's diner, making Thursday her regular day off. "I wish I remembered more about her."

"You were so young," Lydia murmured. "It was so tragic."

Before either of them spoke again, the front door closed with a thud. "Miss Lydia? Are you here?"

Robbie Calloway. Anamaria's muscles tensed. Trust him to find them together; after all, less than twenty-four hours ago, he'd warned her to watch her step with Lydia.

The older woman's expression remained distant, and her response was absently made. "Back here in the kitchen." She was still thinking about the tragedy of Glory's death. Sadness and sorrow tainted the very air around her.

Footsteps sounded in the hallway, then the door swung open and Robbie walked in. Except it wasn't Robbie, but someone who looked and sounded a great deal like him. One of his brothers, Anamaria realized with relief.

He wore a dusty T-shirt with Calloway Construction stamped across the front, along with faded jeans, heavy work boots and a platinum wedding band on his left hand. He wasn't quite as handsome as Robbie, but there was an air of blunt honesty about him. *What you see is what you get.*

Lydia's smile was warm, motherly, as she reached one hand to him. "I was hoping you'd stop by this morning. I caught one of your people about to dig up my lilies in front yesterday. After the chewing out I gave him, he might not be back."

"I told you, Miss Lydia, you've got to quit putting the fear of God into my subs. They're just men. They don't know how to handle a formidable woman like you."

As Lydia responded with a laugh and a protest, Anamaria sipped her tea and quietly observed Robbie's brother. He radiated contentment. He loved his wife, she loved him, and they were having a girl in August. They would name her Sara Elizabeth, after their mothers, but he would insist on calling her Angel.

It was so easy to see into some futures. So hard to figure out a thing about her own.

"Russ Calloway, this is Anamaria Duquesne. She's new in town," Lydia said.

He nodded politely in Anamaria's direction. "You've met the right person to help you get acquainted. Miss Lydia knows everyone and everything that goes on in this town."

Lydia smiled modestly. "Not quite…but I'm working at it. And in that spirit, did you come looking for me just to brighten your day?"

"Of course. And to tell you that the landscape guy will be over here at one, so you can scare him instead of his employee."

She smiled again, looking totally harmless, Anamaria thought, but she *would* scare the guy.

After Russ left, Lydia said, "Those are the flowers your message was about. Mr. John's prize lilies. I have an entire bed of them at home, and I'd transplanted some here. That idiot had his shovel in the ground about to uproot them when I stopped him." Her expression turned serious, and she toyed with the teacup before finally glancing up again. "Do you have… You said there might be…"

"Another message from Mr. John," Anamaria said smoothly. "He's concerned about Kent."

Another harmless message, like the lilies, she thought. But apparently it wasn't harmless to Lydia. She stiffened, her hand frozen above her teacup, and the color drained from her face. As her hand began to tremble in midair, deep sorrow lined her face.

With a heavy sigh, she busied herself for a moment, straightening photos that were already straight, closing the lid on the pastry box, securing the small tabs that held it shut.

Finally she looked at Anamaria. "Kent is my sister's boy. He's a Calloway, for all the good it did him. An only child, born to a man whose standards were impossible and a woman too self-absorbed to be any kind of mother. If ever two people were ill-suited to have children, it was Cyrus and Mary. Harrison and I did what we could for the boy, but no matter how much your aunt and uncle love you, it's still not the same as having your mama and daddy's love...and that's all Kent ever wanted.

"Cyrus is dead now. That was no great loss to the world. And Mary still has a home here, but she spends her time traveling. Paying attention to everyone in her life except the ones that count the most. Do you know she didn't come home when Kent's son was born?" Her eyes glistened with emotion. "Connor was four years old the first time she saw him. She was in Europe when Kent and Connor's mother divorced. She was in Asia when he married Lesley, his current wife. Connor will graduate from high school this May, but Mary won't be there to see it. I hate to speak poorly of my own sister, but..."

But she'd lost the child she loved dearly, while her sister turned her back on her own child. The unfairness of it could cause a saint to turn catty.

"But you and Harrison have been here for Kent. You were here when Connor was born, when Kent divorced, when he married again. You'll be there at Connor's graduation."

Lydia quietly agreed. "We always have been. We always will be." Again, in one of those changes that Anamaria was beginning to expect, she stood and waited pointedly. "This has been a lovely time, but if I'm going to intimidate that landscape contractor, then I need a little time to get ready for him."

By the time Anamaria got to her feet, Lydia was already opening the door into the corridor. "Thank you for the pastries, the tea, the conversation."

At the front entrance, Lydia opened the door, then rested one hand lightly on Anamaria's arm. "We'll see each other again soon. And give my best to Robbie." She nodded, and Anamaria turned to see a familiar figure leaning against the hood of her car. Definitely Robbie, wearing khaki trousers and a pale blue button-down shirt, ankles crossed, hands in his pockets and a hard look on his face.

Her heart rate increased a few beats as she said goodbye to Lydia, then circled around to the side gate. Because of the impending confrontation. Not because he was quite possibly the handsomest man she'd ever known. Not because he might be worth regretting. Simply because he was her adversary.

That was something she couldn't risk forgetting.

Anamaria moved with the assurance of a woman who knew her body and was comfortable in her skin. She came through the gate, then strolled along the twenty feet of sidewalk that separated them, stopping just out of reach.

Just close enough for him to catch a whiff of her fragrance—exotic, musky, putting him in mind of heat and hunger and long sultry nights. There was nothing exotic about her clothes—a denim skirt that ended a few inches above her knees, a white V-necked shirt, its short sleeves cuffed once— but the image, too, filled him with heat and hunger.

She was gorgeous.

"Three men are traveling," she said without a greeting. "An accountant, a doctor and a lawyer. A storm breaks, they have nowhere to stay, so they stop at a farm, knock on the door and ask the farmer if they can spend the night. 'I only have room for two of you inside,' the farmer says. 'The third one will have to sleep in the barn with my pig.' The accountant says, 'I'll do it,' so he goes to the barn. A little while later, he comes back to the house and says, 'Sorry, I just can't stand the smell out there any longer.' The doctor says, 'I'll go,' and he goes to the barn. Soon after, he's back at the house, saying, 'Sorry, the smell is so bad.' The lawyer sighs and says, 'I'll go.' A little while later, the pig comes to the house and says, 'Sorry, the stench is just too bad.'"

Robbie didn't crack a smile. Lawyer jokes weren't overly appreciated in the Calloway family, where about half the adults had law degrees. "River's Edge is closed to the public on Wednesdays."

"I know. Miss Lydia says hello."

"Did she ask you to come here or did you set this up?"

Anamaria gazed at him a moment, all dark eyes and full lips, revealing nothing. "And this is your business how? Oh, right, her husband's paying you to spy on both her and me."

He didn't feel guilty. A lawyer's job was to protect his client. If Anamaria were as innocent as she wanted him to believe, she wouldn't mind that.

"Where's your toy car?"

He gestured over his right shoulder. "In my sister-in-law's parking space." Jamie's office came with one space in the private lot behind the building, but deeming the alley spooky, she never used it. Since he knew the only two tenants who did, he figured the Vette was safe there.

"My car may not be as pricey—or apparently as high maintenance—as yours, but it is mine, so please get off it."

He stood, brushing dust from his butt, then stepped onto the curb beside her just as she stepped off. She didn't go to the driver's door, though, and let herself in. Instead, she headed across the street.

"Where are you going?"

She waved one hand in the air but didn't slow or turn back. "Follow me and see."

It was a nice, sunny Wednesday morning. He had nothing

on his schedule for the rest of the day and had a cooler packed with ice-cold water and sandwiches and his boat waiting at the Calloway dock for an afternoon's fishing—his favorite pastime.

Then he glanced at Anamaria again, at the gentle sway of her hips, the strong muscles of her calves, the swing of her arms—and amended that thought to second favorite. The fish were always biting.

He jogged across the street and caught up with her as she started along the block on the north side of the square. "How is Lydia this morning?" he asked as he matched his stride to hers.

"She's perturbed with one of your brother's subs for messing with her flowers."

He grimaced. He'd once crashed his bike into one of Lydia's flower beds and had spent the better part of the next month doing penance in her garden, digging, hauling rock, weeding. He'd never gone near anyone's flower beds after that. "I suppose you had another 'message' for her today."

She glanced at him as they reached the corner, then turned onto the path that led to Ellie's Deli. Steps led to a broad covered porch, and a screen door opened into the main dining room. Ignoring his comment, she said, "I met your brother."

"Which one?"

"Russ. He seemed very nice. I was surprised."

The waitress greeted them with a smile. "Table for two?"

Anamaria gave him another glance, quick but seeing more, he'd bet, than others saw in twice the time. "Are you going to skulk nearby if I don't invite you to share my table?"

"Calloways don't skulk." Then he added, "Yes, I am. We'll take a table in the back room, Carmen."

Anamaria opened her mouth as if to object, glanced around the dining room, then closed it again. Ellie's was a busy place, the main room nearly full, and more than a few people were watching them. Wondering who she was. Wondering what he was doing with her.

Carmen led them to a wrought-iron table on the glassed-in back porch, set out menus and silverware, then left to get iced teas for them both. Anamaria chose the chair facing out. He sat where he had a great view of brick wall and her.

"How many brothers do you have?" she asked as she spread a white linen napkin over her lap.

For a moment, he closed his eyes, aware of her slow, even breaths and that sweet, exotic fragrance, of warmth and desire and need. When he opened them again, she was giving him a level look. "I was projecting the answer. You didn't get it? Some mind reader you are."

"I don't read minds. I read futures."

Reaching across the table, he held out his hand, palm up. "Read mine."

"No."

"Why not? Am I not gullible enough?"

"Because you're a skeptic. I don't waste my time on skeptics."

"How convenient, to deal only with people who already believe your mumbo jumbo."

She studied him a moment, a cynical smile curving her lips, then opened the menu and turned her attention to it. One instant she was focused entirely on him; the next, she wasn't. The difference was as obvious as turning off a light.

Carmen returned with the teas, delivered a loaf of warm dark bread and soft butter, then left with their orders. Anamaria continued to ignore him. He didn't like it.

"Three," he said at last. "Rick lives in Atlanta, Mitch in Mississippi and Russ here. We look alike, we talk alike, we sometimes act alike, but I'm the charming one."

Finally she shifted her attention back to him. "I doubt everyone who knows you would agree."

"Maybe their wives would argue the fact." Rick's wife, Amanda, certainly would. Jamie might adore him, and Mitch's wife, Jessica, hardly knew him, but Amanda tolerated him only for Rick's sake. Robbie couldn't even blame her. He'd given her plenty of reason to despise him.

"Why aren't you married?" she asked.

"How do you know I'm not?"

She nodded toward his left hand and the bare ring finger. He held out his hand, fingers spread, gazing at it. "Rumor has it that my old man had so much practice at removing his wedding band that he could do it with just his thumb, and so quickly that a prospective one-night stand never even noticed his hand moving."

"I bet he was your hero."

"I hardly remember the bastard. I was five when he dropped dead of a heart attack. I never missed him." He sounded callous but didn't care. "Tell me about your father."

She gave another of those cynical smiles. "Don't disappoint me and tell me you didn't check out my birth records."

He shrugged. "Mother—Glory Ann Duquesne. Father—Unknown. That's officially. Unofficially, did you ever meet him?"

"Not that I'm aware of."

"Did you ever miss him?"

She waited until Carmen had served their meals to answer. "The last marriage in the Duquesne family took place more than two hundred years ago, and the only children born since then have been girls with gifts. Men have little place among us. We have no husbands, brothers, uncles or sons, no fathers or grandfathers. We don't miss what we don't have."

"So your only use for men is to bed them and forget them." Somewhat similar to his own policy for women. He didn't indulge in one-night stands; that would be too much like his father. He preferred pleasant, short-term relationships that ended amicably on both sides. In a town like Copper Lake, with its twenty thousand or so citizens, the "amicable" part was important.

"Not forget," Anamaria disagreed. "The Duquesne women love well."

But temporarily. It sounded as if the two of them were a good fit, on that issue, at least. But the Duquesne women, apparently, made little to no effort to avoid pregnancy. Robbie made every effort. Adults might not owe each other anything after an affair ended, but a baby…that changed everything.

"Are you planning to move back to Copper Lake?"

She shook her head.

"Sell the house?"

Another shake.

"Come back in another twenty-three years for a visit?"

She speared a tiny tomato and a chunk of cucumber on her fork and dipped them in dressing before shaking her head. Her earrings, silver chains that cascaded from a diamond-shaped shield, caught the sun, winking as they swung gently against her neck. "Who knows? I can't tell you what I'll be doing twenty-three days from now, much less twenty-three years."

"Not a wise thing to say for a woman who claims to read the future."

"Not my own future. I rarely see anything about myself or people I'm close to."

"What else do you do? Do you know who's on the phone before you look at the caller ID display? Can you pick lottery numbers?" He made his voice Halloween-spooky. "Do you see dead people?"

A stricken look crossed her face, shadowing her eyes, chasing away the easy set of her mouth and making her lower lip tremble just a bit until she caught it between her teeth.

Robbie felt like an ass. He'd forgotten that her mother had died, that seeing her dead in her casket was likely the most traumatic event in Anamaria's life.

"I'm sorry," he said awkwardly. "I didn't mean…"

After a moment, she smiled, a quiet, resigned sort of gesture. "It's all right. I should have expected…"

What? Tactless questions from him?

"I read emotions. I do numbers and charts. I read palms. I have visions. But people are always fascinated by communication with the dead, even nonbelievers. Everyone's hoping that Grandma will pass on the location of a fortune no one knew existed or that Grandpa will tell them where the casket of priceless jewels is hidden."

"Do they ever?"

She shrugged, unaware that the tiny action made his fingers itch to touch her. To stroke over her skin. To smooth the cotton of her shirt. To brush her neck the way the earrings did.

Or maybe she wasn't so unaware, he thought as something came into her eyes. Heat. Intimacy. Mystery. Though a person didn't need to be psychic to see he found her damned attractive.

"If any of Mama Odette's clients ever struck it rich as a result of her communing with the spirits, I'm not aware of it."

"For a seer, you seem to be unaware of a lot of things."

If his comment annoyed her, she didn't let it show. She was cool, serene. He liked cool and serene.

They ate in silence for a few moments, until voices became audible in the hallway that led to the room. One of them was a waitress; the other belonged to Ellie Chase. She and Tommy had had an on-again, off-again thing that started about five minutes after she'd moved to Copper Lake. They seemed pretty good together, except that Tommy wanted to get married and have kids, and Ellie didn't. Occasionally, Robbie wondered why. Even he wanted kids someday.

Fair-skinned, blue-eyed kids with blond hair, he thought with a glance at Anamaria. He'd always been partial to blondes—icy, well-bred, blue-blood, who could fit into his life as if they'd been born to it.

Conversation finished, Ellie rounded the corner. "Hey, Calloway, who let you in here?"

He shifted in the chair to face her. "Don't bitch, Ellie. I'm one of your best customers."

"I've noticed. All that expensive schooling, and you can't even put a sandwich together."

"Yeah, but I work miracles in the courtroom."

She crossed the small room, her hand extended. "Hi, I'm Ellie Chase."

"Anamaria Duquesne." Anamaria took her hand, a quick shake, a light touch, but more than she'd offered Robbie so far. "This is your restaurant?"

"Every table, every brick and every mortgage payment."

"The food is great."

"Anamaria's in the restaurant business in Savannah," Robbie said, pulling a chair from the next table so Ellie could join them.

"Really? Are you in the market to expand? I'm giving serious thought to selling this place and running away."

"She threatens to do that about once a month," Robbie said.

Anamaria smiled as if she knew the feeling. "So does Auntie Lueena. I work for her, so the headaches are hers. I just show up ready to do what she tells me."

"I love my job. Really, I do." Ellie sounded as if she were trying to convince herself, but Robbie knew it was so much bull. She'd worked damn hard to make the deli a success and had only recently begun the expansion into a full-service restaurant. She *did* love her job. "What kind of place does Auntie Lueena have?"

Anamaria smiled again, soft, affectionate. He wondered if that smile was ever spurred by anyone other than family.

Friends—he was sure she had them. Boyfriends—he was sure she had them, too. Plenty of them. All that she could handle. "It's a small family diner. Soul food. Comfort food. She's been in the same location for thirty years and has had the same menu for twenty-five."

"And you do a little bit of everything?"

"Wait tables, run the register, wash dishes, cook, bake."

Robbie had trouble envisioning her in a hot, busy kitchen, hands in steaming water, prepping vegetables, stirring pots, skin dusted with fine white flour. She was too exotic, too sensual for such mundane activities. She should spend her time lounging on a beach somewhere, wearing beautiful clothes, shopping in expensive stores for diamonds and rubies and emeralds to show off against her luscious skin.

Ellie didn't seem to notice either her exoticness or her sensuality. He supposed, her being a woman, too, that was a good thing. "You ever want a place of your own?"

"No. Not at all." But Anamaria didn't say what she did want. A full-time career telling fortunes? Or did "seeing" people's futures full time require more ingenuity than she possessed? He imagined that on a regular basis it would drain the creative well pretty dry.

"Do you come from a restaurant background?" Anamaria asked.

"No, I—" Distracted, Ellie looked in the direction of the hall, where, an instant later, Tommy appeared around the corner. Right now, judging by the look he wore, if they weren't off-again, they would be soon.

"You ought to put the boy out of his misery and marry him," Robbie murmured.

"Worry about your own love life," she retorted, rising easily from the chair. "Anamaria, it was nice meeting you. Come back soon. I'd love to talk more."

She met Tommy in the narrow aisle halfway across the room. She stopped; he stepped aside. Their gazes held for a moment, their expressions equally blank, then she moved on.

Definitely off-again. Great. Robbie preferred his buddies to be happily attached or happily unattached. Anything in between was too big a pain in the butt.

Tommy watched until Ellie turned the corner out of sight, took a deep breath, then covered the last few yards to the table. "I called the dock and they said your boat was still in its slip, so I figured you'd be here." He tossed a manila envelope on the table. "The papers we talked about."

The case file on Glory Duquesne's death, complete with photographs. Aiming for relaxed, Robbie slid the envelope off the table and onto his lap. "Thanks." He gestured toward the chair Ellie had just vacated, but Tommy shook his head. "Anamaria Duquesne, Detective Tommy Maricci."

One corner of her mouth quirked at his emphasis on Tommy's title. "Detective Maricci," she said with a regal nod.

He cocked his head to one side, studying her a moment before saying, "You look familiar. Have I arrested you before?"

Chapter 3

Anamaria couldn't stop the laughter that bubbled free. "Not yet. But there's still time." Mimicking Robbie, she waved one hand lazily at the empty chair. "Please join us, Detective."

This time he did so, swinging the chair around to straddle it. "You can call me Tommy."

He was about Robbie's age, an inch or two shorter and probably twenty pounds heavier, all muscle. Black hair, dark eyes, olive-skinned, with a stubble of beard on his jaw that gave him a slightly disreputable look. He didn't need the badge or the pistol on his belt for his air of authority; he came by it naturally.

The sorrow hovering around him, though, wasn't natural. A new hurt having to do with Ellie Chase, an old one connected to his mother. Anamaria couldn't tell if Mrs. Maricci was dead; she wasn't sure Tommy knew himself. But wherever she was, in this life or the next, she wasn't *here* and hadn't been for a very long time.

"So you're in the psychic business," Tommy said.

"And let me guess—you're in the skeptic business."

"Nah. He's skeptical enough for both of us." He jerked his head toward Robbie. "Besides, my great-grandma Rosa was from the old country, and she was a big believer in the evil eye and spirits and all that. Are you setting up business here in town?"

"My visit here is nothing more than that. A visit. A break from Savannah."

"And yet the first thing you do is call Lydia."

Who'd told her husband, who'd told his lawyer, who'd told the local cop. "If you don't believe me, Detective, feel free to keep an eye on me."

He glanced at Robbie. "It might get kind of crowded."

So Robbie had already made clear his intention of doing just that. She didn't mind. She'd been viewed with suspicion and distrust before, and would be again. She shifted her gaze to Robbie. "And here I thought it was just coincidence running into you outside River's Edge this morning," she said sweetly.

"No, you didn't," Robbie replied bluntly. "You knew when I left your house yesterday that you'd be seeing me again."

That she would see him, and have no regrets about him when she left. Whether that meant sleeping with him—or not—she didn't yet know.

Whether it meant trusting him—or not—was still a question, as well.

She picked up her purse and reached for the ticket the waitress had brought with their food. Robbie slid it out from under her fingers and switched it to his other hand. She smiled faintly. She could insist on paying for her share of the meal, but there would be other, more important things to argue about than a salad and half a sandwich.

"Thank you." She stood, and her denim skirt fell into place, the cotton of her shirt shifted, and two appreciative male gazes watched. She offered her hand. "It's a pleasure meeting you, Detective."

His hand was warm, his grip strong but restrained. "Let's do it again without him."

She thought of Ellie Chase, doing one of the thousand daily jobs vital to the running of the restaurant, and the way he'd looked at her when she'd walked away from him. He would be a safe choice for a spring affair—handsome, sexy, totally in love with another woman. Her heart might break for him, because she suspected if she got to know him, she would like him very much, but it wouldn't be broken *by* him.

Still holding his hand, she bent close, her mouth almost brushing his ear. "As if you aren't already taken," she murmured. "But if you need a friendly ear or a soothing tonic, you know where to find me."

When she straightened, Robbie's gaze was narrowed, not quite forming a scowl but definitely hinting of something territorial, something…primal. As safe as Tommy was, Robbie was twice that dangerous.

He followed her to the cash register near the front door, paid the tab, then they walked outside. He held the envelope under one arm while putting on a pair of dark glasses. She had sunglasses in her purse, big ones that Mama Odette called her movie-star glasses, but she didn't bother with them. Perhaps it was the Cuban in her, or the Haitian or the African, but she loved the sun, bright and hot. Loved the air heavy with moisture and the lazy, languid way it made her feel.

"Do the contents of that envelope concern me?" she asked when they'd walked half a block in silence.

"Why would you think that?"

"Oh, gee, I don't know. Your client asks you on Tuesday

to look into my background, and on Wednesday your detective friend shows up with an unmarked envelope of 'papers' you talked about. Call it…"

"A premonition?" he supplied drily.

"Intuition."

He didn't respond but followed when she turned in midblock and jaywalked to the square. The paths there were shaded by giant oaks and were sweetly scented by the plantings along the edges. She was wondering what he would do if she simply slipped the envelope away from him. Would he take it back or let her look inside? Could there be anything inside worth seeing? Her financial history? Her arrest report? The legendary permanent record that had followed her from kindergarten to twelfth grade?

She knew all those details of her life. Seeing them in official report format didn't interest her.

"Tommy's not available," Robbie said abruptly.

"I saw that."

"You mean—"

"Even a blind man could see the emotion coming off the two of them. What's the problem?"

He shrugged, obviously unwilling to share. "What did you say to him?"

She shrugged, too, equally unwilling to share.

In only a moment, they were approaching her car. She would have walked longer with him. If he offered a tour of downtown, or even the whole town, she would accept. It was a beautiful day, the air fresh with promise, and there was something about walking with him—being with him—that filled her with promise.

But he wasn't making any offers.

She unlocked her car, then opened the door to disperse the heat collected inside. "Thank you for lunch."

"You're welcome." He held out his hand, and for a time she simply stared at it.

His voice was taut when he spoke. "You shook hands with Ellie and Tommy. You can damn well shake hands with me."

She continued to stare. His fingers were long and lean, hinting at power. The nails were short, the skin tanned, with a few old scars and a callus here and there. They were hands that could arouse and soothe and protect, that could hurt but wouldn't. Hands that could shake her world so thoroughly that nothing would ever be the same again. *She* would never be the same again.

Her own hands stayed at her sides. "Touching can be a very casual thing," she said softly. "It can also be very powerful. Very hurtful. Very healing." She paused, moistened her lips, debated the wisdom of her next words and said them anyway. "Come home with me. I'll touch you there. Not here."

For an instant, time stopped. Then anger turned to passion, heat suffused his face, and for an instant his hand trembled, brought to a stop immediately when he clenched his fingers into a fist. He took a step back, opened his mouth, but didn't say anything.

What was he thinking? That his demand for a handshake was certainly no invitation to seduction? That she was too bold for his tastes? That she was arrogant to think he wanted her in bed? Or that Calloway men didn't sleep with women of questionable reputation?

For generations, Duquesne women had been lovers of such men, had carried on their affairs in secret and birthed their daughters with no help, no money or even acknowledgment from them. Mama Odette speculated that Anamaria's own father was just such a man.

Anamaria had never thought she would be drawn to a man

who found her unsuitable because of the color of her skin or the life she'd been born into—because of who she *was*—but here she stood.

Robbie took another step back, then dragged his fingers through his hair. "Jeez. I haven't been speechless since I found out that my brother the cop was marrying a stripper." And here he was, the successful lawyer, fielding a brazen seduction offer from a con artist.

She could tell him the offer stood. She could let him believe her only intent had been to shock. She could tell him it was inevitable, if they kept seeing each other, if nothing cooled this ardor between them.

Her smile formed slowly, growing until it was full and sly, looking as real as she knew it wasn't. "In a lawyer, 'speechless' is a good thing," she said, her voice huskier than usual. She pulled on her sunglasses, then slid behind the steering wheel, gazing up at the dark-tinted view of him. "I'm sure I'll see you around."

He was still standing in the street when she drove away. She wasn't sure as she watched him in the rearview mirror whether she'd saved herself from a huge mistake.

Or made one.

Robbie wasn't sure how long he stood there—long enough for his brother to come along, thumping him on the back of the head as he came up from behind.

"I know Mom taught you not to play in the street despite Rick's and my best efforts to convince you otherwise," Russ said, not breaking stride until he reached the sidewalk.

His scalp stinging, Robbie took the few steps necessary to bring Russ into punching range, then shoved him on the shoulder. "I'm not ten years old anymore. Quit hitting me."

"I've been hitting you since you were old enough to

understand the threat implied in 'Don't tell Mom.' Why would I stop now?"

"Jeez, I don't know. Because I'm thirty-two freakin' years old, maybe?" Robbie asked snidely. "Where are you going?"

"To see my wife." Russ gestured to Jamie's office, down the block twenty feet and across the corner.

"I'll walk with you. My car's in her parking lot."

"What were you doing in the street?"

Wondering what the hell was wrong with him. Why he hadn't gotten in his car—hell, gotten in Anamaria's car—and gone home with her. It wasn't the first time a woman had come on to him, but it was the first time he hadn't jumped at the chance. Anamaria was gorgeous. She was hot. The way she looked, the way she moved, the way she smiled... He choked back a groan.

He must have made some sound, though, because Russ frowned at him. "You okay?"

"Yeah." Just nuts.

"You working today?"

"Yeah. Sort of." Technically he was—Harrison Kennedy had asked him to keep watch on Anamaria. He could take her up on her offer, have incredible sex and get paid for his fun. Normally, the possibility would amuse him, but he was having trouble thinking clearly today. Lack of blood flow to the brain, he figured.

On the sidewalk outside Jamie's office, Russ stopped. She was standing behind her desk, flipping through a stack of papers. He tapped on the glass, and she gave him the kind of smile that could cut a man off at the knees.

No woman had ever smiled at Robbie that way, as if he'd brightened her world merely by being part of it. There had been a few who'd gotten close, but he'd ended things with them before it could develop any further, because he'd never come close to feeling that way about them. He expected that someday he would. It had happened to Mitch. To Rick. To Russ. Odds were, it would happen to him.

And, no, damn it, he was not going to think about black hair, liquid-chocolate eyes or powerful touches.

Jamie held up two fingers, and Russ nodded, then leaned against the brick building. "Two minutes, my ass. The more pregnant she gets, the slower she gets. By the time this kid pops, her mama's going to be slow as a snail." He didn't look annoyed, though. He was so excited about the baby that no one could stand him besides Mitch, who had one daughter and another on the way. "We're having lunch at Ellie's. Want to go?"

"I've already eaten." With all the restaurants in town, of course they were going to the deli today. Ellie would give them about five minutes to order, and then she would tell them about him being in there with Anamaria, along with a description that would detail everything down to the color of polish on her toes. Then Russ would know at least part of the reason he'd been standing in the street like a dumbstruck moron.

Shoving his hands in his pockets, he claimed another portion of brick. It retained the heat of the morning sun that had moved overhead. "Do you remember a family who used to live here named Duquesne? Mother and daughter?"

Russ rubbed his jaw thoughtfully. "Anamaria Duquesne? I met her today."

That was right. She'd been surprised that Robbie's brother would be nice. "You don't remember her from twenty-three years ago?"

Russ snorted. "Jeez, I was eleven. If I couldn't hook it on a line, shoot it, tackle it or beat it up, I wasn't interested. How do you know her?"

Robbie shrugged.

The casual effort didn't fool Russ or stop his grin. "There

was a time when the sight of her could have left me standing in the street, too, with my tongue hanging out."

"It's just a case," Robbie said sullenly, irritated by how accurate his brother's description was. Okay, so his tongue hadn't been hanging out literally. Figuratively, it had, and damned if Anamaria hadn't known it. That big wicked smile before she'd covered her eyes with those ridiculous glasses…

"Oh, man, are you gonna get in an ethical dilemma here?"

"I don't have ethics."

Russ snorted again. "You're not half as superficial as you want people to think."

His brother was giving him credit for being a better person than he really was. Among their branch of the family, Robbie was the superficial one, the shallow one, the irresponsible one. He was the one who'd taken most advantage of the family name, the one who'd really believed that Calloways *were* better, privileged, entitled. While he'd dated a lot of women, the only ones he'd taken seriously were just like him, with family money, influence and social standing.

He'd never gone out with a black woman. Never been involved with a woman whose occupation was less than respectable. Never dated a woman he wouldn't want to introduce to his family and friends.

But Anamaria hadn't asked him for a date.

She'd offered him sex.

And he hadn't taken her up on it. Didn't know if he could say yes. Didn't know if he could say no.

"Is she a client or an adversary?" Russ asked.

"You're a lawyer, too. Don't ask me questions."

"I have a law degree," Russ corrected him. "I've handled only one case, and you know how that turned out."

He'd handled his own divorce. Bad idea, Robbie had tried to tell him, but Russ hadn't been in the mood to listen to his irresponsible kid brother. It had taken losing half of everything he owned and three long years for him to forgive Jamie for representing his ex-wife. And look at them now.

Not wanting to look at them now, as Jamie came out of the building, Robbie dug his keys from his pocket. "Hey, Jamie."

He bent and she pressed a kiss to his cheek before sliding her arm through Russ's. "Want to have lunch with us?"

"No, thanks. Have a good time."

He picked up the Vette, drove home and stretched out on the couch before opening the envelope. Glory Duquesne's life might have been full, but the folder regarding her death was pretty thin. Reports from the officer who'd been assigned the call and the detective who'd investigated, a witness statement from the fisherman who'd found the body and the autopsy report—a significant event summed up in a handful of pages. If not for the photographs, the file would have been depressingly flimsy.

He hadn't seen many dead people who hadn't already been prepared for viewing, so he wasn't sure what to expect from the photos. They were clear, color, glossy shots, exactly what Harrison had described: a woman lying at the foot of the riverbank, snagged on branches. There was a gash on her forehead, but the night's steady rain had washed away the blood. She looked as if she might have been sleeping, except for her position—half in mud, half in water.

But she wasn't sleeping. She was dead. And twelve hours before, her belly had been swollen, heavy with a baby, a living, breathing child who'd needed only to be born to live on her own. To be born anyplace besides half in the river to a dying mother.

The last photograph wasn't from the scene. It was Glory alive and laughing outside the AME Zion church. He was vaguely familiar with it—knew the land it sat on had once been Calloway land, that most of its members had worked for one Calloway or another at some time in their lives. It was a neat white building, the grass around it trimmed and green. Other people stood in the background, but the camera's focus was on Glory and Anamaria.

The mother wore a pink dress—hot pink and fitted, not quite what he'd expect of a psychic/fraud but exactly what he'd expect of a woman who liked the attention of men. A straw hat shading her face from the noonday sun, she smiled brightly as she held her daughter's hand.

Anamaria's dress was pink, too, but the color was paler, more delicate. Her straw hat was white, with pink ribbons that streamed down and tangled in her hair. She was grinning, her cheeks chubby, her eyes sparkling, and she was missing a front tooth. In her free hand, she clutched a small Bible, the edges of a crayon drawing sticking out.

One pretty woman, one destined to steal a man's breath. One dead, the other very much alive.

He turned back to the notes and began reading. The first contact with the police had come not from the fisherman but from the elderly neighbor babysitting Anamaria that evening. Glory had promised she'd be home by eight; there'd been no sign of her by eight-thirty, and her hysterical daughter insisted that something was wrong, that her mama was in the water. The babysitter was a believer, the dispatcher was not.

There had been another call at ten, another at midnight, both brushed off. Then the fisherman had called in shortly before six the next morning.

That baby's crying that her mama's in the water. She's scared to death, and she's making herself sick. You've got to do something.

Do you see dead people? he'd asked Anamaria over lunch, making a joke of it.

I have visions, she'd replied.

He hadn't believed her. It was so easy to claim parapsychological abilities, and so hard to prove. So easy to prey on people who were vulnerable, seeking peace, trying to ease a loss, and so easy to dismiss anyone who was less gullible as a nonbeliever. *I don't waste my time on skeptics,* Anamaria had said.

But according to the police dispatch tapes, she had known her mother was in the river at least ten hours before Glory was found. How? Could she have seen a vision of Glory's death?

He'd find it easier to believe that she had literally seen Glory in the water. The river ran just behind the trees that bordered the Duquesne house, less than two hundred feet away. Maybe she'd gone on that walk with Glory—or sneaked out and followed her—and had seen her mother fall. Or maybe she'd even caused her to fall...

Either way, psychic vision or real life, how traumatic would such a sight have been for a five-year-old?

After rereading the witness statement, he returned the file to the envelope, laid it on the coffee table and got to his feet. He was halfway to the door when his cell phone rang. Harrison Kennedy's name on the caller ID display made him grimace, but he answered.

"You know, the girl met with Liddy this morning."

"Yeah, I know."

"What did they talk about?"

"I don't know, Harrison. There were only two people there. Anamaria's likely to tell me it's none of my business or to ask Lydia, and you told me not to ask Lydia anything." He let himself into the garage, opening the door as he settled in the Vette's driver's seat, then switched the phone to speaker as he backed out. "Have you asked Lydia?"

"She said they talked mostly about her mother."

"Lydia's mother?"

Harrison sounded impatient. "No. The girl's mother. Why would they talk about Lydia's mother? Marcette's been dead for years."

Why would they talk about a white-haired man and flowers the first time? Robbie thought irritably. People didn't go to psychics to get messages from the living.

"Lydia says she's here to find out more about her mother. Says she's curious. She didn't ask for any money, but she said something to Lydia that made her...I don't know. Sad. Worried."

Why are you here? Robbie had asked, and Anamaria had smiled. *Because I used to live here.* She'd added other reasons: she was resting, retreating, taking a break from her regular life.

He hadn't believed her about that, either. If her purpose for coming to Copper Lake was as simple as a vacation, why had her first act been to contact Lydia? Why had she asked to meet with her a second time? He supposed even scam artists needed a break from time to time, but a few slick tricks with Lydia here could pay for a real vacation somewhere else.

"Did you ask Lydia why she was sad?"

"She acted like it was nothing. Just that the girl made her think about the mother."

The girl had a name, and so did the mother. Was it asking too much for Harrison to use them? "She did see Glory regularly for a year," Robbie reminded him. "Some people might consider that a basis for friendship."

"I have no doubt Lydia liked the woman, but they weren't friends. Lydia was a source of income for her. Nothing more."

Maybe. "Will you change your mind about letting me talk to her?"

"No. I don't want her upset any more than she already is."

"Look, I've got to go," Robbie said as he turned into the riverfront parking lot. "I'll be in touch with you soon." He disconnected before Harrison could say anything else and got out of the car.

He didn't usually walk along the river if he had a chance to be out on it instead. Before Jamie had gotten married, they'd met here at least once a week to exercise her mutt and talk, but she and Mischa were taking their walks with Russ now. Sometimes Robbie missed her. They'd been close for years. She was the one person he'd told almost everything, but her marrying Russ had changed things. Now she was family, and her focus was on a different Calloway.

Not that he begrudged Russ being happy. God knows, after the hell Melinda had put him through in their marriage, he deserved every minute with Jamie.

There were a few joggers out, a few mothers with their children. Giving them a wide berth, Robbie turned north, following the path through the grassy park and along the high bank of the Gullah. It was a slow river, wide and lazy. He'd fished in it, swam in it and raised hell on it with his brothers and his buddies. He'd brought girls to its banks to make out and cracked more than his share of beers in a boat on hot days, and he'd never known that Glory Duquesne and her baby had died in it.

It didn't take long to reach the place where Glory had been found. The pavement had ended, giving way to a hard-packed dirt trail that ran along the top of the slope above the water. This section was used by mostly joggers; Tommy ran a few miles along the trail every day.

Robbie slowed at the pilings that marked a dock long since rotted away. According to the police report, Glory had been tangled by the gnarled roots of a fallen oak twenty feet north. Much of the tree had rotted away over the years, but the trunk, easily three times his own girth, remained on the shore, unaffected by weather or time.

He stared down at the water's edge. Had Glory been conscious after her fall? Had she tried to push herself up out of the mud and muck? Had she known her baby was coming? Or had life ended for her when she'd hit her head? Consciousness gone, lights out, unaware that she and the baby were doomed to die.

A shudder worked through him, and he rubbed his arms, bemused by the goose bumps. No doubt, Anamaria—or especially her grandmother, who claimed to talk to the dead— would say something still lingered here from that night. But he wasn't sensitive to the living; he damn sure wouldn't feel anything from the dead.

He gazed downriver, then up, to orient himself. The path continued to the north, narrowing, angling away from the river and into the trees. It ended before reaching his uncle Cyrus's fishing cabin, about a mile and a half upstream. Also between here and there, a short distance to the east, was Easy Street and the Duquesne house.

It was a seven-minute walk at a good pace before the first sign of habitation came into sight: a house, battered and tilting, that would have blended into the surrounding forest if not for the lemon-colored sheets on the clothesline out back. He counted four houses—a roof here, a flash of sun reflected off a window there—before he followed a beaten path through the woods to the street.

Anamaria's house was thirty feet to the left, her car parked in the driveway. A dog barked down the street, quieted by an admonishing *hush*. The voice was elderly and came from the porch of the nearest house. With rusted screen enclosing the porch and the roof creating deep shade, he couldn't see the woman who had spoken, but he did hear her next words. "I been telling them kids to quit using that path. Look what's done stumbled in on it from the river. It's a Calloway."

A moment's silence, expectant, damn near humming in his ears. Then... "It certainly is. Thank you for your time, Miss Beulah."

The screen door creaked, and Anamaria came down the steps, avoiding the hole in the third one. She crossed the dirt and pine needles that passed for a yard, then stopped in the street a dozen feet in front of him.

"What's the difference between a dead rat lying in the road and a dead lawyer lying in the road?" She paused only a moment. "There are skid marks in front of the rat."

When he didn't smile, she did and began walking lazily toward her house. He forced his feet to move, to walk beside her rather than behind her, where he could watch the sway of her hips.

"Did you decide to take me up on my offer?"

Yes. No. Damned if I know. Silence was a good choice when you didn't know what to say, Granddad Calloway had always advised. It was Robbie's choice as they moved single file past her car, then climbed the steps to the porch. As he reached the top, though, his mouth opened and words came out of their own accord.

"Were you at the river the night your mother died?"

Anamaria's fingers curled around the screen door so tightly that the nail beds turned white. She turned, forcing him to stop on the last stair, blocking his way. The extra height put her an inch or two above him and allowed her to stare down at him with all the ice she could muster. "What?"

He moved as close as the step would allow, his shirt brushing hers, his face mere inches from hers. "According to the police report, you told your babysitter that your mother was in the water hours before she was found there. Were you there?"

She never retreated. Never. But that afternoon she did, taking a step back, folding her arms protectively over her middle. She tried to look away, but his blue gaze was too intense, tried to walk away, but her body refused to obey.

He closed the distance between them again, standing much too near, intruding on every breath of her personal space. "*Were* you at the river that night? Did you sneak out and follow her, or go looking for her? Were you with her when she fell? Did you know she was dying? Did you leave her there?"

Sensation threatened to overwhelm her: his heat, his scent, his arousal—oh, yes, even though he was questioning her, he was aroused. So were her own emotions. Sweat beaded on her forehead as chill bumps raised on her arms. Over the buzzing in her ears she heard whimpers coming from the front bedroom, felt her five-year-old heart breaking all over again, tasted the fear, the helplessness, the anger that Mama wasn't there to help her deal with what she couldn't understand.

She grabbed onto the anger, straightening her spine, wrapping it around her for warmth and strength. "Who the hell do you think you are, coming here demanding answers from me?"

He raised his hand, bringing his fingertips close to her cheek, so close she felt their warmth, so close she imagined their texture, smooth and calloused, against her skin. Every nerve ending was humming, every pleasure sensor on alert, waiting, anticipating, but he stopped before making contact. Stopped. Stared at her. Said quietly, deliberately, "I'm the man you're going to touch."

Her heart beat a hundred times before she managed a breath. The whimpers faded back into the dark corner of her memory, and so did the anger. A knot of fear remained, though. The unbridled passion experienced by Duquesne women was a powerful thing, according to Mama Odette. It would take away her breath, rip out her heart and make a different woman of her, one who understood the exquisite pleasure and pain of desire, love and loss.

It was her destiny. Since she was a little girl, she'd grown up expecting not marriage but a broken heart. She envisioned it. Was resigned to it. Had waited for it all her life.

I'm the man you're going to touch.

She was. Maybe not this instant. Maybe not today. But soon. When the mere promise of a touch could made her tremble…definitely soon.

And then he would break her heart.

She dragged in another breath, turned away and walked into the house. The windows were open in every room except the front bedroom, and the gentle breeze floating in from the kitchen was scented with cocoa and butter and coconut, ingredients in the cookies she'd made to take to her neighbors. She didn't need to hear quiet footsteps to know that Robbie followed her. She felt his presence. Felt his gaze on her. Felt his ambivalence toward her.

He knew he would break her heart, too. He preferred his lovers well-bred, educated, sophisticated, elegant. He liked women who blended in at the country club—fair-skinned, blond, blue-eyed—who understood the value of influence, appearances and convention.

But he wanted *her.*

At least for sex.

At least for a while.

She went into the kitchen, fixed two glasses of iced tea and set them on the table, then peeled the plastic wrap from a plate of cookies and put it in the middle. She sat in one chair, crossing her legs. After a moment, he sat in the other, and for a long time, that was all they did. Sit. Avoid looking at each other. Ignore both tea and cookies. It wasn't as uncomfortable as it should have been. At least, until she spoke.

"No," she said at last, with a great breath for fortitude. "I wasn't with my mother that night. I didn't literally, physically, see her in the river."

The breath he exhaled was as strong as the one she'd taken in. "Then how did you know?"

"I had a vision. It was as real as if I *was* there. I could hear the rain falling. I could feel the drops stinging my skin. I could smell the mud and the river, and I could see…" Her fingers knotted in her lap. "I called to her. I pleaded with her to open her eyes and come home where she belonged. I screamed at her, but she didn't hear me. She was already gone."

The clock on the wall counted the seconds, one for every two beats of her heart. Sixty of them had ticked past when she added, "It was the first vision I ever had."

Another sixty seconds passed before he met her gaze. He didn't believe her. That was all right. She knew what she'd seen, knew it was real. His cynicism didn't change that.

Finally he took a drink from the sweating glass in front of him. Moisture collected on his fingertips, wiped away carelessly on a napkin. "You said you don't see anything about the futures of people you're close to."

"I said rarely. But it wasn't Mama's future I was seeing. It was her death." She gazed out the window, thinking idly that she needed to hire someone to cut back the weeds before they grew over her head, smiling faintly at the thought of a lawn service making routine visits to Easy Street.

Then, feeling Robbie's gaze, she turned back to him. "Detective Maricci gave you the police report, didn't he? That's what was in the envelope."

He didn't reply. Protecting his source.

"Can I see it?"

Her request startled him. "Why would you want to?"

"She's my mother. I want to know how she lived. I want to know how she died."

"She died alone," he said flatly. "In the dark. In the rain."

Anamaria shook her head hard enough to make her hair sway. "She wasn't alone. My sister was with her, and there were others waiting for her—her grandma Chessie, Chessie's grandma Moon, Moon's grandma Florence. And she liked the rain."

Glory *had* liked the rain, Anamaria realized as soon as she heard the words. They'd gone for walks in the rain, leaving the umbrellas and slickers at home, splashing through every puddle they came across, quacking like ducks and laughing till their faces hurt. She *remembered*.

Across from her, Robbie was scowling. "Lydia says you're here because you're curious about your mother. Why didn't you tell me that when I asked?"

Half a smile curved her mouth. "I'd met you all of two minutes before. I didn't owe you an answer."

"If you didn't have anything to hide…"

"If you hadn't come expecting the worst of me…" She let the smile form fully. He still wasn't convinced. It was apparent in the way he looked at her, the very air around him. And she still didn't owe him an answer, but she decided to give him one anyway.

"Your father's death wasn't even an inconvenience in your life. My mother's death changed my entire life. She *was* my life. I lost her. I lost my home." She brushed her hair back before settling both hands on the tabletop. "Don't get me wrong. I've had a great life. Instead of one mother, I had a dozen—Mama Odette, Auntie Lueena and Auntie Charise and their daughters. They taught me everything I needed to know about being a girl, a woman, a Duquesne. They explained the visions to me. They helped me develop my sight.

They were there when I went on my first date, when I graduated from high school, when I had my first client, when I suffered my first broken heart."

Not that it had been much of a break. She'd been seventeen, left for an older woman of twenty, and for two weeks she'd stayed in her room and cried as if she were vying for the title of drama queen of the universe. Her first day back at work at the diner, a handsome construction worker had flirted with her, and within another two weeks, she'd hardly been able to remember her ex-boyfriend's face.

"They were great mothers," she said quietly.

"But they weren't *your* mother."

She was touched that he grasped the difference. "I don't remember much about living here. I know I must have been very happy, because I know how *un*happy I was when I first went to Savannah. Mama and I must have sat at this table for our meals. She must have tucked me into bed at night, and I must have crawled into bed with her when the storms came. We lived our lives in this house, just the two of us, but I don't remember."

"What does it matter?"

Spoken like someone who'd never had a doubt about his history, himself.

Silently she nudged the plate of cookies in his direction. When he shook his head, she took it to the kitchen counter, covered it once more with plastic wrap, then glanced at him over her shoulder. "It matters. It matters to me, and it especially matters to Mama Odette."

Chapter 4

In his job, Robbie made a lot of decisions based on whatever sketchy information he had: whether a client was being truthful, whether he could create reasonable doubt in a jury's minds, whether he could trust the story a witness was telling him. Instinct said Anamaria wasn't being entirely truthful.

But he didn't know whether it was real instinct or if, as she'd said, he'd come expecting the worst of her. He was a lawyer. He'd seen the worst of a lot of people. He'd come by his distrust honestly.

Truthfully, though, it didn't matter whether he believed her. Distrust alone wasn't going to keep him away from her. It wasn't going to keep him out of her bed.

She was leaning against the kitchen counter, hands resting on the chipped laminated top. She could go to church or appear in court in that outfit, but it still struck him as damn sexy. The skirt was neither tight nor short, but it made him focus all too much on the curves underneath it—the flat belly, the rounded hips, the long muscled thighs. The T-shirt was substantial enough to reveal only a hint of the bra underneath, and it fitted no more snugly than the skirt, but it was enticing all the same. Soft, but not as soft as the skin it covered. Concealing, on a body that should be revealed.

He turned his chair to face her, then hooked his arms over the ladderback. "Why does it matter to Mama Odette?"

Anamaria shrugged. "Mama wasn't her only daughter, but she was her favorite. She wants to know about the last days of her baby's life. According to the doctors, she's in the last days of *her* life. It's made her sentimental. Wistful."

He hadn't been raised by his grandmother. He probably hadn't seen her more than once a week throughout his life, and most of their visits had been brief conversations before or after a meal. She hadn't been nearly as influential in his upbringing as Granddad Calloway, but when she was gone, he would miss her deeply. He couldn't imagine the loss Anamaria would feel when her grandmother passed on. What had she called herself? *Mama Odette's girl*, with a wealth of affection in the words.

"Why doesn't she ask Glory herself? You said they talk."

"It doesn't work that way, at least, not for them. My mother is a facilitator. She delivers messages to Mama Odette, but not for herself. Not for us."

"Why not?"

"Because that's the way it is, chile." Her accent was heavier, the sounds slower and more rounded. How many times had she asked her grandmother for explanations? How many times had Mama Odette given that answer?

It wasn't much of an answer, in Robbie's opinion. Anamaria looked as if she found it acceptable. He liked proof. She took things on faith.

"What's wrong with her?"

Her eyes widened, and his jaw tightened a notch. He might be a skeptical, lazy bastard, but Sara had taught him and his brothers common courtesy. It had taken a long time, but the lessons had stuck.

"Besides being almost seventy, her heart is giving out. The doctors thought she wouldn't survive this last heart attack, but she's holding on."

"Doctors don't know everything."

Unexpectedly she smiled. "One thing we agree on. Where is your car? Were you afraid to be seen driving down my street after having lunch with me in town?"

Something uncomfortable twitched at the back of his neck. Guilt, shame—emotions Calloways didn't often deal with. Life was easier when you were better than everyone else and owed apologies to no one. Of course, they weren't better than everyone else, but as long as they didn't acknowledge it, they didn't have to deal with it.

At least he could truthfully say this time that being seen had had nothing to do with his decision to walk there. It was seeing that had mattered, and what he'd wanted to see couldn't be seen from a car. "I wasn't intending to come here. I went for a walk along the river." No reason to tell her that he'd gone to the place where her mother's body was found, or that he'd continued walking to see if it was conceivable that a five-year-old could have made her way from this house to that slope on the river and back again on her own.

She could have. The path that had brought him from the river to Easy Street was a straight shot, a few hundred feet, with no wrong turns to take. It had been in use so long that the dirt was packed as solid as pavement, so it was likely Glory and Anamaria had taken it at some point. Anamaria had probably been familiar with it.

Though Glory's car had been found in the parking lot in town. How would her daughter have known to find her along the river path? And if she hadn't known, why would she have set out that way alone in the night in the rain?

Still, it was a more logical scenario than the alternative: that she really had seen a vision of her mother's death.

Without moving a muscle, she tensed. "It was in the police report, wasn't it? The place where she was found."

He nodded.

"I've been meaning to walk out there."

"Will you know it when you see it?"

She shook her head. "But I'll feel it."

"I'll go with you."

"So you can gauge my reaction? So you can determine whether I've been there before?" Her tone was mild, the shake of her head chastising.

"Who's the skeptic now?" He paused. "I assumed you wouldn't want to go alone, but if you'd prefer it…"

"No," she said quickly. "Thank you."

"You want to go now?"

She glanced out the window over the sink, and he looked, too. The air had gone still while they talked, the breeze dying until not even a leaf stirred. Thin white clouds streaked across the sky, and the sun shone with an intensity that turned its rays white-gold and harshly illuminated everything in its path.

"It's going to rain," she murmured, shaking her head. "I don't think I could bear it in the rain."

He checked the weather every morning, just in case he could get out on the river, and today's forecast was for sun, high clouds and temperatures in the midseventies. Not even a drop of rain was expected until the weekend. But if she was more comfortable with an excuse to avoid the river trail, that was her prerogative.

Leaving the chair, he carried his glass to the sink. Closer to her, he could smell the cookies, the coconut and almond flavorings and that exotic fragrance, fainter now, that was her. He stood so close that she would have been justified in putting half the room between them, but she didn't move. She simply looked at him.

Reaching past her, he lifted the edge of the plastic wrap, took out a cookie, then nudged the wrap back in place. When he withdrew, his sleeve brushed along her bare arm. Not even real contact, but the closest they'd come, and it burned along his skin as if it were real.

Her breath caught, a tiny gasp, but her gaze never flickered from his. He stepped back, then took another step, when all he really wanted was to press her against the counter, wrap his arms around her, crawl inside her.

He forced himself to take a bite of the cookie, chocolate with oatmeal and pecans, forced himself to turn and follow the hall back to the living room doorway. The room looked fifty years old, as if Glory had bought the place already furnished and hadn't changed a thing. The furniture was heavily worn, the sofa covered with a bright African-print throw, the chair with a faded quilt. Holes in the walls marked where drapery rods had been attached above the windows, but now only blinds covered the glass, the old-fashioned kind with wide metal slats.

"Good cookie," he murmured when she stepped into the doorway to watch him.

"Thank you. When you work in a restaurant kitchen, you learn a few things."

He circled the room, gazing at an empty bookcase, a shelf designed to display knickknacks and a TV stand that held a bouquet of wildflowers. "Why did Glory move here?"

"Mama Odette says she had wanderlust. Some of our

people do. Duquesnes have wound up in Ireland, Japan, Cuba, Haiti and all across the U.S. Glory's first love was in South Carolina. The second lived in Texas."

"What about your father? Where was he from?" Could he be from Copper Lake? Someone Robbie knew? Worse, someone he was related to? That was only half the damn county.

She shook her head. "Mama was living in Atlanta when she got pregnant with me. I was a few months old when we moved here. Mama Odette says she chose Copper Lake because it was close to her friends in Atlanta but close enough to go home when she needed."

Mama Odette says... Too bad that she remembered so little herself, that virtually everything she knew about her mother was filtered through someone else. He couldn't imagine having only secondhand knowledge of his mother. To have missed out on all the years he was supposed to have with her, and to have forgotten what little time they did have together...

Passing her, he crossed the hall, came to a closed door and opened it. Small room, faded pink walls, bare bulb above a single iron bed. "Your room?"

"Yes." She came no closer than the hall, and a shudder rippled through her. "If I go in there, I'm afraid I'll hear her still crying."

"Her?" he echoed, then returned to the hall. "You. When you were five."

She nodded.

Real image or psychic vision, whatever she'd seen that night had had a hell of an impact on her. He couldn't blame her for staying away for twenty-three years. Couldn't blame her if she'd refused to return now. But if Mama Odette was anything like Grandma Calloway, no one refused her anything. If she wanted every last detail leading up to her daughter's death, she would get it. No matter the cost to her granddaughter.

The next room down the hall was the bathroom and, beyond that, another bedroom. Big windows, lots of light. Inexpensive but sturdy furniture. Another iron bed, this one made up with white sheets, white blankets and a dozen white pillows. There was white eyelet lace on the sheets, pale pink flowers embroidered on some of the pillowcases, even paler cross-stitch and ribbon work on others. This was a bed for a woman who knew how amazing she looked in white—and how much more amazing it would be with someone there to appreciate it.

A half-dozen candles sat on the dresser, another half-dozen on the night table. Even unlit, they gave off a fragrance sweet and mouth-watering. A few pieces of jewelry lay on a crocheted cloth on the dresser, alongside a bottle of perfume and a small silver filigree frame. He picked it up, studying the photograph it held. Mama Odette, nearly as round as she was tall, her broad face split by a smile of pure joy. In one arm, she held a little girl, maybe two years old, and the other was wrapped around Anamaria, probably ten years younger, who was smiling, too, a bright sunny look.

"Mama Odette," she explained unnecessarily, then tapped the little girl's face. "Little chile and—" her neatly rounded nail moved to her own face "—big chile. We tease that she calls all of us that so she doesn't have to remember our names."

It would be so easy to catch that finger, to slide his hand up to hers, to pull her against him or to lead her across the room to that white bed. But she'd touched Tommy and Ellie and God knows who else in Copper Lake. He wanted her—needed her—to touch him first.

To take the responsibility for what followed from him? the cynic in him wondered. So he could say, "Yeah, I had sex with this totally inappropriate woman, but she started it"?

By the time they finished, it wouldn't matter who'd started what.

It was a matter of ego. She'd touched the others voluntarily but refused him the same courtesy. He wanted it.

He slid the frame free of her hand and returned it to the dresser. There was nothing else in the room to look at but her. He tried to imagine walking into the annual spring dance at the country club next month with her on his arm. Inviting her to dinner with his mother and grandmother and all the Calloways, the decent, the snobbish and the worthless. Taking her to meet his brothers and their wives, or to the clubs and parties where his friends hung out.

The images wouldn't form. Where did that put him among the decent, the snobbish and the worthless?

"I should go."

"I can give you a ride to your car."

He was about to say no, thanks, when the breeze stirred, rattling the blinds, bringing with it the scent of rain. The sky had gone dark, and a sheet of rain was traveling across the woods and into the backyard, approaching with an increasing patter. He gave her a look before they both moved to the windows, closing them. "Is predicting weather one of your talents?" he asked drily.

"No. I just had a…an idea."

A vision. Nah. It was Georgia. Rains came and went with great regularity. With a one in two chance of being right, it wasn't a tough prediction to make.

"I believe I'll take you up on that ride."

She nodded, then went to close the kitchen windows. He secured the one in the bathroom and was locking the ones in the living room when she came to the door.

The front porch was cool, mostly sheltered from the rain. At Beulah's house, chimes swayed in the breeze, a pleasant tinkle that could grow annoying really fast. Anamaria remotely unlocked her car, took the steps two at a time and hustled inside the car. He followed a few seconds behind, getting wet enough to require a change of clothes when he got home but not nearly as wet as he would have liked for her to be.

She didn't need directions to Gullah Park, so the trip passed in silence, the air between them too close, too heavy. She parked beside the Vette, the only other vehicle in the lot, and waited.

"Have you talked to Marguerite Wilson?"

She shook her head.

"She's the neighbor who was babysitting you the night... I can find out where she's living now, if she's living, and we can see her tomorrow if you want."

"I do. But you don't have to—" She broke off, then managed a faint smile. "Thank you."

He got out, got into his own car, then watched through the rain-streaked glass as she drove away. *Don't thank me yet.* His motives were selfish: Harrison was paying him to keep an eye on her, he still didn't trust her, and he wanted to sleep with her. No reason for her to feel grateful to him.

Not now, maybe not ever.

By Thursday morning, all sign of the rain was gone. The sun had dried the ground, and the narrow ditches that lined Easy Street were empty, drained into the river. Anamaria left her house at ten to meet Robbie at the shopping mall a mile east of downtown, wearing a dress that had enough stretch in its pink-and-black cotton fibers to fit snugly from shoulders to knees. Her sandals were pink, too, like the band that held her hair back and the bangles that encircled her right wrist.

She hadn't taken any extra care with her appearance because she was seeing Robbie. It was a dress she wore often, both for its colors and for its comfort. It hadn't even crossed her mind that men always looked twice at her when she wore it, or that Robbie, already looking twice, might be persuaded to do more than look.

No, she hadn't thought of that at all.

When she'd returned home the afternoon before, she'd looked up Marguerite Wilson in the phone book and found plenty of Wilsons but no Marguerites. According to Mama Odette, the babysitter had been an old black woman who'd lived one street over. Anamaria had visited more than half of the houses in the neighborhood before Robbie had shown up yesterday—no Wilsons there, either. Not a single person, in fact, who remembered her mother.

The mall fronted Carolina Avenue, and the Vette was parked alone on the row nearest the street. She pulled in beside it, got out and locked her car. Robbie had reached across the seat to open the passenger door by the time she'd turned.

Two facts assailed her as she settled into the leather seat: Robbie's vehicle was much smaller, and therefore occupants sat much closer than in her car, and his cologne in that small, confined space was amazing.

"What do you say about a lawyer up to his neck in quick-sand?" she asked, setting her straw bag on her lap after removing her sunglasses. "Not enough quicksand." She didn't wait for a response—or nonresponse—from him. "How much trouble was it finding Marguerite?"

"Enough that you owe me at least a dozen cookies," he replied as he backed out of the space. "Actually, as soon as I mentioned her name to Tommy, he knew. She lives across the hall from his grandfather at the old folks' home."

"So I owe Tommy a dozen cookies." From the corner of her eye, she watched a muscle clench in Robbie's jaw, the same territorial response she'd seen yesterday at the deli. "I don't remember her. Logically, I know someone took care of me while Mama saw her clients and went on dates, but I don't recall. Mama Odette met her only once, when she and Auntie Lueena came up from Savannah to pick me up, and she said she was old even twenty-three years ago." She smiled faintly. "With Mama Odette, though, *old* is relative."

"Not in this case. Marguerite Wilson is ninety-six, so she was seventy-three when your mother died. Brave woman to be taking care of a five-year-old."

"I was a sweet five-year-old. Can you say the same?" When he opened his mouth, she interrupted. "Without lying?"

He gave her a sour look before turning off Carolina. "Sweet gets boring after a while. My brothers and I were never boring."

Would he get bored with her after a while? He was such a product of his upbringing and environment that her differences appealed to him now, but how long before he lost interest? Before he started looking at the well-bred, blue-eyed blondes from the country club in a new light?

She would survive. Duquesne women always did.

"How is Mama Odette?"

"She's fine," she replied absentmindedly, then pulled her gaze from the neat middle-class houses they were passing to look at him.

"I bet you call her every day."

"Twice a day usually. Morning to say hello, night to say good-night."

"Morning to be sure she made it through the night, and night so you can always say goodbye." He slowed and turned into the nursing home lot before responding to her look. "I used to call my granddad every morning and every night."

And when Granddad had passed, he'd had the comfort of having said *I love you* one more time.

With a knot in her throat, she got out and looked around. Morningside Nursing Center was a low brick building with a parking lot across the front and a tall chain fence on three sides. Flowers grew in window boxes, and the grass was green, smelling sweet from a recent mowing.

Robbie joined her at the rear of the car, a bouquet of roses in hand. His cheeks reddened at the look she gave them, and he shrugged before thrusting them into her hands. "Every woman likes flowers."

Especially ninety-six-year-old women who likely hadn't gotten many in their lives.

Marguerite Wilson's room opened off a back hall. Large windows let in a view of a garden, where several residents sat on benches or in wheelchairs, talking, playing cards or just enjoying the morning. Marguerite was sitting in an armchair, a Bible open in her lap, a game show on the television mounted above. She was tiny, with white hair pulled back in a bun, her skin unlined, the angles of her face ageless.

She didn't look familiar. No memories roused, no tickle that Anamaria had ever known her.

Anamaria knocked at the open door, then pitched her voice louder. "Miss Marguerite, can we come in?"

She glanced their way. "There's no need to holler. My hearing's much better than my eyesight," she said with a chuckle. "Come on in."

Anamaria led the way, drawing a wooden chair closer to the old woman and sitting primly on its edge. "I'm Anamaria Duquesne, and this is Robbie Calloway." Holding out the flowers, she lowered her voice and said with a wink, "He brought you these. You'd better watch out for him. They say he's a charmer."

Arthritic hands accepted the bouquet, fingers stroking gently over the creamy petals. "A woman my age don't need the charm. Just the flowers would do the trick." After breathing in the roses' scent, she fixed her gaze on Robbie. "Calloway, huh. I've worked for a few Calloways and known a few others. Some people think they're all bad because they got money and power, but shoot, they're just like any other family. Some good, some bad. Which are you?"

"I'm a little of both," he replied.

Marguerite laughed. "If you'd told me you were all good, I wouldn't have believed it. You're too young and too handsome to not have a little bit of sinning in you."

Slowly she turned her faded gaze back. "Anamaria Duquesne. My, you've grown up."

"You remember me?"

"Even an old woman doesn't go through a night like the last one we shared and then forget it. You look a bit like her, you know—your mama. You're prettier than she was, and that's saying a lot because that Glory was a pretty girl. All the men thought so."

"Were there a lot of men?"

Marguerite tilted her head to one side and smiled. "Oh, they were drawn to her like flies to honey. She was so lovely and friendly and *alive*. She loved people, loved life, and people responded to that, both men and women."

"Who was the baby's father? Did she ever tell you?"

"Wouldn't say." The old lady raised one finger in admonition. "Not *couldn't*. She didn't know who your daddy was, but she knew this one. She just kept it to herself, all private-like. Had her reasons for doing so, but she kept them private, too. I always thought he might be married. Some of her men were. Or he might be white. Some of them were that, too." She sighed softly. "There was men who would pass her on the street as if they'd never seen her before, then sneak off to see her in secret. I told her she should have more pride than to lay with a man who was ashamed to acknowledge her in public, but she just laughed. She said it wasn't what they felt that mattered. It was how *she* felt, and she wanted what she wanted."

What will be, will be, Mama Odette always said.

Glancing at Robbie, who'd taken a seat at the foot of the hospital bed, Anamaria wondered if the events of their lives really were fated or if it was just a rationalization for their lack of restraint. Was she destined to have an affair with him, or should she fight the attraction?

"Do you remember the names of any of these men?" he asked.

"Oh, goodness. There were so many. Black and white, young and old, single and married. I doubt Glory kept track of them all herself."

Marguerite ticked off a dozen names on her bony fingers, thought about it, then added a few more. None of them meant anything to Anamaria, though Robbie reacted to the last one. "Really?"

Once again, the old lady raised that admonishing finger. "Men of God are not immune to temptation."

"They should at least make an effort."

Her smile was full of age and wisdom. "You can make all the effort in the world and still give in. A woman can be as wrong for you as it's possible to be, but if she's in your heart, it's a battle you're not going to win."

"And was Glory in his heart?" he asked.

Another smile, this one mischievous. "No. Just his pants. That one, he gave in so often that he was tempted right out of the pulpit." Her gaze flickered over their heads, and she picked up the television remote control. "My show's about to come on. Come back tomorrow, and we'll talk more. A little earlier this time."

"We'll do that," Anamaria agreed as she got to her feet. "Can I put those flowers in water for you?"

The old woman gazed at the roses. "No. I'd like to keep them close right now. The nurse will do it later." She pressed a button on the remote, and a soap opera theme song filled the air.

Anamaria and Robbie left her to her show. When they reached the hall, he hesitated. "Give me a minute, will you?" After her nod, he went into the room across the hall. "Hey, Pops," she heard him say before the closing door blocked the conversation.

She felt conspicuous, left to stand there while he visited Tommy's grandfather alone. The polite thing would have been to invite her inside, to introduce her to the elderly man or to at least have given her the chance to say no, thanks.

Had her mother truly not minded when men had refused to acknowledge her in public but had been more than willing to share her bed? Anamaria's best guess would be that she hadn't. Glory *had* loved life and had lived it on her terms. A few great passions, a few heartaches and a fine appreciation for love, family, men and sex—that was how Auntie Charise described her sister's life. Those few words described every Duquesne woman's life, and in another few generations, Duquesnes as yet undreamed of would probably remember Grandma Anamaria that way.

Would they suspect that for a time she'd wanted more?

Turning away, she paced off the tiles to the front entrance, pivoted and was halfway back down the long hall when Robbie rounded the corner and started toward her. Her pulse quickened, but she pretended not to notice, stopping in the center of a black tile, waiting for him to join her.

"How is Mr. Maricci?" she asked as he drew near.

Faint color tinged his cheeks. "He's fine."

She almost said, *I would have liked to meet him.* But having to ask took the pleasure out of it.

They left the building, and the air immediately turned warmer, smelled sweeter, felt freer. As nursing homes went,

Morningside might be a good one, but nothing changed the fact that it was a place where people went to die. There was an inherent sadness about it, echoes of lives long ago ended and spirits passed on.

Robbie came around to unlock her door first. She stood, fingers curled around the sun-warmed metal, and met his gaze over the roof of the car. "Was Glory having an affair with the pastor of our church?"

"No. With the pastor of *our* church. I don't remember much about him. Just that he stayed a while, then was gone. I'd have to ask Mom for the details."

Another visit she wouldn't be invited along for. She didn't mind. She *couldn't* mind. It was just the way life was. "Great. So my mother slept around *and* got a minister run out of town."

Robbie frowned as he slid into the driver's seat. "You don't know that," he said as she took her own seat. "Like Marguerite said, he gave in to temptation a lot. Besides, what's wrong with enjoying sex? I like it just fine."

Suddenly warm, she cranked the window down a few inches as he pulled out of the parking lot, and the wind rushed across her fevered skin and whipped her hair. She caught it in one hand, closed her eyes and tilted her face to enjoy it.

Damn, but she was gorgeous, Robbie thought, stealing glances at her from the corner of his eye. The old lady had been right: he had more than a bit of sinning in him, and right now he wanted to do it all with Anamaria.

In secret.

And that was a problem.

It was a few minutes after eleven, and since he hadn't eaten breakfast in longer than he could remember, he was ready for lunch. He didn't ask if she was hungry, too, but took the backstreets to the edge of town, then turned north on River Road.

When they came to the brick-and-iron fence that marked the

beginning of Calloway Plantation, she twisted in the seat to look. Both sets of elaborate gates were open, each driveway a straight shot through a yard the size of six football fields. Even at a distance, the Greek Revival house was clearly visible, with its massive brick columns and three stories of blinding white paint. The oldest live oaks in the county grew on either side, nearly obscuring the row of reconstructed slave quarters.

Uncomfortably, Robbie shifted in his seat, pushing the gas pedal until the needle hovered ten miles over the limit. He wished she hadn't noticed the house, or seen the Calloway name, or caught sight of the slave quarters. He wished she wouldn't say anything, and for once, she didn't.

Their destination was a shabby little town ten miles north, consisting of a convenience store with a post office occupying one small corner, a competing gas station across the street and a ramshackle restaurant perched on stilts over the river. He could count on one hand the women he'd dated whom he could have brought here, but instinctively he knew Anamaria wouldn't mind. "It doesn't look like much, but they've got some of the best food around."

She smiled as they got out and started across the gravel parking lot toward the building. "That's what people say about Auntie Lueena's. Of course, it's not this isolated. It's a given that if you go there, you're going to be seen."

His temper flared because inside he knew it wasn't just a craving for catfish that had made him choose the place. "That isn't why—"

She breathed deeply. "Hmm. Hush puppies. And sweet potato pie. Promise me good creamy slaw, and I'll be in heaven."

"It's creamy," he said grudgingly.

The waitress greeted them and asked about his brothers, his usual companions, then showed them to a booth where the window looked down on the lazy brown river. They ordered, and Anamaria sipped her sweet tea for a time before finally meeting his gaze.

"That's some house. The photographs don't do it justice."

He felt as if, name aside, he should deny any claim to the plantation. The Calloways who'd built it had been dead nearly two hundred years. Robbie had never lived there and never would.

But he'd spent practically every weekend of his childhood there. Family dinners, holidays, reunions. His parents had gotten married in the gardens out back, along with his aunts and uncles and most of his older cousins. His grandma loved lavish weddings and had been disappointed when Mitch, Rick and Russ had opted for smaller, less formal ceremonies. She regularly pestered Robbie to carry on the family tradition and marry there, and he'd always figured he would. Though right now, even the idea seemed wrong.

"Does your family live there?"

"My grandmother. After Granddad died, she moved into the guest cottage on the east side of the gardens. About half my uncles wanted to move into the big house, but she opened it to the public instead." His smile felt more like a grimace. "They weren't pleased."

"What about you? Were you hoping to live there someday?"

"Good God, no. What would I do with eight bedrooms, six bathrooms and a ballroom, all filled with antiques that may have been made for many things but not comfort?"

"You could fill those rooms with children."

An image popped into his mind of little girls with cocoa-colored skin and big dark eyes, with bright, wide smiles and missing teeth and a penchant for pink. Pretty little mixed-race girls living in the house built by slave labor, running through the halls where generations of white Calloways had ordered about generations of black slaves and servants and playing, as Robbie and his brothers had, in the slave cabins.

Cyrus Calloway would turn in his grave. So, probably, would his contemporaries in the Duquesne family.

"Thanks, no. When I get married and have kids, I'll consider a house. Until then, the condo is fine for me."

She gave him a knowing look. "You're not the first person I've met whose ancestors owned slaves, and I'm not the first person you've met whose ancestors were slaves."

No, but she was the first one he'd wanted to have sex with. Besides, there was just something about seeing the grand mansion and the tiny miserable cabins with Anamaria sitting at his side.

"So where did you grow up if not at Tara?"

He waited as the waitress set platters in front of them, then unrolled his silverware from a paper napkin. "My parents' place is back toward town, though it's still on the property. When I was a kid, you could see across the field to Granddad's house, but they've let the trees grow up since then."

"Did your mother remarry after your father died?"

"No. Being married to him was miserable enough that she didn't want to try again."

Her smile was a far cry from the picture he had of her with her mother. It barely touched her mouth, curving the corners just a little, and looked wise beyond her years. "You can't let one broken heart keep you from living."

"Do you speak from experience?"

"Not my own. My family's."

"Sounds like your mother was probably the one breaking the hearts." Like mother, like daughter.

"She broke her share, I'm sure. Suffered her share, too." After a moment's silence to sample the catfish on her plate— *Excellent,* she murmured—she asked, "Has your heart ever been broken?"

"Once." At the time, he'd thought he would never get over

it, now he had trouble recalling the woman's face. "I was twenty and stupid. Or is that redundant? I was thinking marriage. She was thinking fun with as many guys as possible. She dumped me, I drank a lot, got into a lot of trouble and eventually got over it."

"Do you still drink a lot?" She didn't sound wary—didn't look it, either. She might have been asking something as insignificant as whether he still worked.

"No." He paused, then admitted something he'd never acknowledged before. "I'm a mean drunk. After Rick just about broke my face last time, I decided that since I couldn't control my behavior while I was drinking, then I'd have to stop the drinking."

"That's not an easy thing."

"No," he agreed. It had been eighteen months, and he still missed the booze. His mouth still watered, and he still caught himself thinking, *Just one drink. What could it hurt?* But he hadn't given in yet.

Deliberately, politely, she changed the subject. "It must have been nice growing up with three brothers."

"You have two sisters."

"But we never lived together. We didn't get to know each other until we were teenagers. We're close but not the way we would have been if we'd been raised together."

"Why weren't you?"

She ate for a moment before shrugging. "Mama was sixteen when Lillie was born. Lillie's father was ten years older. He had money and a wife who couldn't have children of her own and who didn't mind raising someone else's baby. Jass's father was older, too, with a good job, a close-knit family and a strong conviction about living up to his responsibilities. He wanted to marry Mama, but she said no. When he wanted to take Jass, though, she said yes." She smiled faintly. "And then there was my father, who apparently couldn't have cared less about Mama or me."

"He may not even have known you exist."

She gave another careless shrug. "Maybe not. It doesn't matter."

Someone else might have doubted her, but Robbie didn't. His own father's absence from his life didn't matter, either. Gerald dying when he did had been a good thing for Robbie and his brothers, and God knows, Sara's life had improved. Whatever she'd felt for Gerald in the beginning, in the end she'd been happier without him.

Robbie didn't want to be happier without someone he'd once loved and had kids with.

Anamaria pushed her plate away, caught the waitress's eye and ordered a slice of sweet potato pie. When the waitress glanced at him, he shook his head. Watching Anamaria eat would be dessert enough for him.

The silence that settled around their table was close and comfortable. She sat, arms crossed loosely beneath her breasts, and watched the river, and he sat, watching her. She was aware of his scrutiny—he could see it in the faint smile that played over her mouth—but she didn't mind. She let him look all he wanted.

But it wasn't enough. He couldn't help but wonder how much *would* be enough.

Or, with Anamaria, was there even such a thing as *enough?*

Chapter 5

The trip back to Copper Lake was quiet, followed by another journey along its backstreets. Anamaria gazed out the window, thinking about secrecy and temptation and pride, before she recognized the car next to them as hers. Glancing around, she saw that they were at the mall, that Robbie was waiting for her to get out of the car. She forced a smile as she opened the door. "Thanks."

"You're welcome."

"You don't have to go with me to see Marguerite tomorrow."

His shrug was impossible to read. *Not a problem, I'm happy to go, I'm happy to not go.*

"I'll see you."

He nodded, muttering something that she barely heard as she got out of the car. *Soon,* she thought, but she couldn't be sure.

Soon, she knew anyway. Destiny or foolish desire, he wouldn't stay away. She didn't want him to.

With a wave, she got in her car, started the engine, rolled down the windows and drove away. He was still sitting there when she caught her last glimpse before distance and traffic blocked him from sight.

She returned home on Carolina Avenue and River Road, driving through the heart of downtown. She let herself into the house, left her purse on the chair just inside the living room doorway, then went to the kitchen to pick up a straw bag filled with plastic-covered plates of cookies. There were still houses in the neighborhood to visit, people to meet who might have known her mother. Though people regularly came and went in her Savannah neighborhood, there were also plenty of people who'd lived all their lives in those few blocks. This neighborhood wasn't likely to be any different.

When she turned to take a bottle of water from the refrigerator, something crunched beneath her feet. Glass, shards of it, dotting the floor, the rug in front of the sink, the countertop.

The window above the sink had been broken, the brick that had done it looking incongruous against the white porcelain. With goose bumps rising, she concentrated on the house but felt nothing unusual, no sense of danger, no threat.

In her bedroom she found two shattered windows, two bricks. The bathroom window, small and narrow, was intact, though one window in each of the two front rooms also was cracked.

Juveniles? Vandals choosing victims at random? Or a warning from someone who didn't like her questions?

Back in the kitchen, she located the local phone book that had come with her new phone service and dialed the nonemergency number for the Copper Lake Police Department. The dispatcher wasn't particularly interested in the call. Petty vandalism, especially in her neighborhood, wasn't a high priority what with *real* crime going on.

Twenty-three years ago a five-year-old girl hysterical over her missing mother hadn't been a priority, either.

She was about to hang up and start looking for a repairman when the dispatcher put her on hold. Almost immediately, Tommy Maricci came on the line.

"Hey, Anamaria, this is Tommy, Robbie's friend. We met yesterday. What's up?"

"Someone delivered five bricks through my windows while I was out this morning. I was just checking to see if it was worth my time to make a report."

"I'll be over in a few minutes. You need a glass man? I can call Russ on my way and get someone."

For half an instant, she considered refusing. A few broken windows didn't need the attention of a detective, and she was perfectly capable of finding someone to replace them herself. But if knowing Robbie could get her both a detective and a repair guy that easily, why not?

"That would be great. Thanks."

"You're not in the house, are you? If someone's hanging around—"

"They're not. I can feel it."

He might have smirked, but he didn't say anything cynical. "I'll be there in a couple of minutes."

"Thanks." She hung up, then gazed at the fragments of glass still in the window frame. The house had stood empty for twenty-three years with no problems, and now, four days after she'd moved in, this had happened. What a coincidence.

Except that she didn't believe in coincidence.

At least it didn't appear that the vandals had come inside. There was little to steal: a colorful wardrobe. A supply of cosmetics and perfumes. An array of cast-off dishes and pans from the diner. She'd brought nothing of value with her besides—

Rushing into the bedroom, she tugged the suitcase from the closet shelf, then heaved a sigh of relief. The wooden chest remained in its corner, untouched since she'd placed it there Sunday evening.

Her heart was slowing to a normal beat when car doors slammed outside. She went to the door, opening it as Tommy Maricci came up the steps, accompanied by a uniformed female officer. "Detective," she greeted him.

"You can call me Tommy."

"First names could make it awkward if you arrest me."

"Nah. I'm on a first-name basis with most of the people I arrest. This is Bonnie DeLong. She's going to look around."

She nodded to the woman, a petite brunette who projected an air of confidence. Size aside, she could take care of herself, or at least did a good job of making people think she could.

"We don't get many calls to this street," Tommy said as he followed Officer DeLong inside.

"Don't get them? Or don't answer them?" Anamaria asked.

His gaze was level. "Easy Street's a pretty quiet place. Miss Beulah next door and Mr. Gadney at the end of the block keep an eye on everyone around here, kids and adults both."

So he knew something about the neighborhood. She was impressed, and just a little chastened.

Leaving Tommy and Officer DeLong talking, Anamaria went out to the front porch and sat in a chair, the creak in its rockers soothing in the warm afternoon. A few minutes later, Tommy joined her, a notebook and pen in hand.

"How long were you gone this morning?"

"I left at ten and got back a few minutes before I spoke to you on the phone."

"Where did you go besides the nursing home?"

She looked at him, and he raised both hands in a mock defensive gesture. "Pops never has been able to keep a secret. Miss Marguerite, either."

But Robbie could.

"I had lunch at a place called Joe Bob's."

Tommy made a note of that. "It used to be Joe & Bob's," he said conversationally. "Brothers. But the *and* fell off the sign, and they never replaced it, so now it's just Joe Bob's. Alone?"

The sudden question was intended to catch her off guard, and it almost worked. She opened her mouth to answer but asked her own question instead. "Does it matter?"

"Only if we find a suspect and it turns out he was with you the whole time. Though Robbie heaving bricks through the windows is about as likely as Miss Beulah doing it."

She didn't respond. Apparently, going to such an out-of-the-way place for lunch wasn't enough to keep people from talking. Robbie's caution had been for nothing.

"Bricks are hell to get fingerprints off, but we'll try," he went on. "The grass is beaten down around back and on the sides. Bonnie's gonna see if it leads to the woods or the street. After yesterday's rain, there might be a footprint or two, but I wouldn't count on it. Unless the goober happened to drop his wallet out of his pocket, we probably won't find out who it was. By the way…" He eased his wallet from his hip pocket, flipped it open and pulled out a handful of business cards. The top one he handed to her, then after sorting through the others, he offered her a second one as well.

The first was his, with numbers for the police department, the detective division and his cell phone. The second belonged to a yard service. "They do good work for a good price."

"Is that a hint, Detective?" she asked with a smile.

"Half the punks in town could hide in this yard. If

someone's going to come sneaking around here, at least make it harder for them."

She folded her fingers around both cards. "I'll give them a call."

They sat in silence for a moment, the only sounds the squeak of her chair, a bird in the live oak and the occasional growl of distant thunder. The afternoon sun was bright, casting sharp-edged shadows, and the air was heavy, typical of a Georgia spring day. The far-off storm might roll through or might dissipate completely. Either way, the warm afternoon would turn into a warm evening, full of sweet scents and promise.

Would she spend it alone?

Officer DeLong came onto the porch, the screen door banging behind her, and gave her report: The bricks were like a million other bricks in the county; there were no footprints; and the trail through the tall grass disappeared into the woods. "Probably kids," she said. "Sneaked in from the woods."

Anamaria knew she was wrong about the first part. Whoever had paid her a visit probably had come from the woods, but the senseless innocence of kids playing vandal didn't hover in the air. Still, she thanked Officer DeLong before Tommy sent her on her way.

When he showed no inclination to leave, Anamaria asked, "What do you know about my mother's death?"

"Only what's in the file."

"The file you gave Robbie?"

He didn't flush, look away or show any other signs of guilt. "Yeah."

"The officer who found my mother—is he still around?"

He shook his head. "It was a guy fishing who actually discovered her. He died probably ten years ago. The officer who got the call moved away while I was still in high school, and the detective who caught the case is gone, too. Retired eight, nine years ago, and left town."

She stopped rocking, crossed her legs and folded her arms over her middle. "What about the baby? Is there any chance..."

"That she survived? That somebody pulled her from the water and decided to keep her?" He shook his head. "You don't just keep kids you find. People notice. They ask questions, especially when a baby that's disappeared is in the news."

Anamaria nodded in agreement. Mama Odette had never sensed anything one way or the other about the baby, and Glory didn't know, either. There were some who believed babies had no spiritual connection to the living until their births, that those who died at the time of birth returned to heaven unknowing of their family on earth. Mama Odette believed the trauma of death, leaving the world at the same time her baby came into it, had kept Glory from knowing Charlotte's fate.

Anamaria didn't know *what* she believed.

An approaching vehicle drew her attention to the street. A pickup truck pulled to the side behind Tommy's police car, and a rotund man in a sweat-stained T-shirt climbed out. He took a toolbox from the bed of the truck before starting toward the house.

"That's one of Russ's guys," Tommy said. "He's going to replace those windows."

"I appreciate it."

He met the workman outside and disappeared around the corner with him. When he returned alone a few minutes later, he came no farther than the top of the steps. "If anything else happens, call me. And if you need a friendly ear, you know where to find me."

She smiled at the echo of her words to him the day before. "I'll keep that in mind."

* * *

Robbie left the Eleanor Calloway Public Library shortly after three with a list of names, courtesy of the city directory from twenty-three years ago: every family that had lived on Easy Street, Tillman Avenue and the surrounding streets. Some he recognized as still living in the local area; others were unfamiliar to him. It shouldn't take long to find them on the Internet—or, easier still, to turn them over to Tommy and let the police department do the looking.

He'd just unlocked the Vette when a '72 mint-condition Chevy pickup stopped behind him. Wearing a Calloway Construction cap and looking hot and grimy, Russ raised one hand in greeting. "Don't you ever go to the office?"

Robbie walked back to the truck. "Not if I can help it. Don't you ever stay in the office?"

"Not if I can help it." Russ gestured toward the brick building. "Haven't you heard? The Internet has made the library obsolete."

"Not entirely. Where are you headed?"

"To the Hobson site. Gotta fill in for one of my guys. He's doing some work over at Anamaria Duquesne's house. Apparently, someone used her windows as targets."

Robbie's muscles tightened. Why would anyone break her windows? And why had his brother found out before he had? Hell, even if she'd called the police first, she should have called him second, and Tommy should have called him, too.

Oblivious to Robbie's silence, Russ went on. "Hey, you want to come to dinner Saturday night? Mom's coming, and Rick and Amanda will be in from Atlanta. You can even bring a date if you can get one."

Anamaria's image formed much too quickly, and so did a picture of his family. Even though he couldn't think of another woman he wanted to spend an evening with, he just couldn't merge the two images into one. "I don't know. I'll see."

"Yeah, well, let us know or just show up. There's always plenty of food." Russ shifted into gear and, with a nod, drove away.

Robbie remained where he stood for a moment. He believed in looking ahead and being prepared. He wasn't prepared to fall in love with a woman so different from himself. He wasn't prepared to be part of a relationship that came with all the usual problems and then some.

He wasn't prepared to deal with prejudice that would affect any children he had.

Did that make him prejudiced as well?

Or just weak?

Frowning, he walked back the few feet to his car. He had intended to go by the office next, but instead he headed for Easy Street. As soon as he drew close, he identified the white Calloway Construction pickup parked on the street. Then he saw Anamaria, standing at the end of the driveway, talking with Lenny Parker. He eased his foot off the gas, slowing to little more than a crawl, and watched as she extended her hand and Lenny took it.

Annoyance rumbled through him. When was the last time he'd been jealous over a woman? He couldn't recall. He didn't want to be now. Didn't want to give a damn who she touched or that she didn't touch him.

But he did.

She let go of Parker, and he got into the truck, waving as he pulled away. He repeated the gesture a moment later as he passed Robbie.

By the time he'd parked behind her car, she'd climbed to the top of the steps. She still wore the black-and-pink dress that fitted like a second skin and made him think about nothing but taking it off her. Her hair swayed in the breeze as it freshened, bringing with it the lush scents of the woods, the muddiness of the river and distant rain, and her gaze remained on him, steady and calm.

"Why doesn't a rat bite a lawyer?" she asked, waiting a beat before answering, "Professional courtesy."

He took the steps one at a time, stopping on the second, so close that only the faintest breath of muggy air separated them. "Why didn't you call me?"

"I called the police."

"Why didn't you call *me?*"

She hesitated before replying, "I would have told you." Not necessarily today, maybe not even tomorrow, but at some time she would have mentioned it to him.

A good enough answer…but not the one he wanted.

He stared at her, and she stared back. It was hot and sunny, and he swore the hairs on his arms stood on end, as if the very air were charged with energy and arousal. He moved to close the inch between them, and she took a backward step onto the porch. He followed. She retreated. Across the porch. Into the house.

She backed away until the living room door frame was at her back and he stood so close at her front that their clothing brushed with each breath, hers shallow, his ragged. He rested one hand, just inches from her head, on smooth wood, the other on papered wall, and leaned in until he could feel the soft puffs of her breath, could see the rapid beat of her heart, could smell the nearly faded fragrance that floated around her. "Why—" his voice was barely audible above the thudding of his own heart "—didn't you call me?"

She stared at him, her eyes big enough, dark enough, intense enough, to get lost in. Then she answered softly. "I knew you would come anyway."

Wind blew through the open windows, cooling his skin, making him realize that he burned hot from the inside out. Heat radiated from her, too, her skin gleaming and damp, tiny strands of hair clinging to her forehead. Thunder vibrated through the house, and the lightning that followed fed the sparks that arced around them.

"You wanted me to come," he said, his gaze locking with hers.

A tiny nod, then the words, "I needed you to."

Needed. He hadn't needed a woman since he was twenty, and that hadn't been need so much as immaturity, possessiveness, familiarity, expectations. He didn't need now. He could leave. Could put space between them. Could walk out the door, get in his car and drive away as if nothing had ever happened. As if it might not kill him.

He didn't *need* to stay.

But he wanted to.

Another gust of wind rustled through the house, stirring his hair. She raised her hand as if to brush it back but hesitated, her fingers unsteady between them. He couldn't breathe, couldn't move, couldn't look at anything but her fingers, couldn't want anything but her fingers on him. Stroking him, holding him, arousing him.

And finally, finally, she touched him. Her fingertips brushed through his hair, something his mother and grandmother had done dozens of times since he was a child, simple, innocent.

And so damn intimate that he hurt with it.

She smoothed his hair back, then slid her hand along his cheek, his jaw, his throat, so lightly that he might have imagined it. Abruptly, her fingers curled up a handful of his shirt, and her other hand was there, as well, pulling him hard against her as she rose onto her toes and kissed him.

Anamaria couldn't say she'd given much thought to their first kiss—who would initiate it, how the other would receive it, whether it would be sweet and gentle, or hello or goodnight or goodbye. All she'd known was it would come sooner or later. Be welcomed, sooner or later.

It scorched her head to toe, sensitized her skin and revved her heart into a thundering rush. Every breath was hot and hungry and smelled of Robbie. She was absorbing him through her skin, her pores, the very air that seeped into her lungs. In the course of that one sweet, greedy kiss, tongues entwining, bodies pressing together, fever rising, she recognized him as the real reason fate had brought her to Copper Lake.

He was her destiny. Her broken heart.

But as he slid his hands around to cup her bottom, to lift her against his erection, she didn't care. Broken hearts healed. She could try to protect herself by sending him away, but he would come back and she would welcome him. And she would survive, as Glory had survived. As all Duquesne women survived.

She was only vaguely aware of moving along the hallway, of stepping out of her shoes, of pulling his shirt free of his trousers. His belt gave way with a tug; his zipper slid open with a yank. They bumped into something—the doorway, she thought dimly—and then they were in her bedroom, bright with sunshine and cooled by the breeze coming in the open windows.

Less than seventy-two hours, a voice whispered in her head. That was how long—how little—she'd known him. Less than three days. Too soon to be kissing him like this. Too soon to be intimate.

Destiny doesn't care about time. That voice was Glory's, filled with laughter and life and always, always hope.

And Mama Odette's: *When it's time for somethin', it's time. You can't hurry it along, no more than you can stop it flat-out. That's just the way it is, chile.*

Her and Robbie. Right now. Just the way it was.

He drew back, taking a breath, and she did the same. They were both barefooted, their breathing loud and uneven in the quiet room. His pants hung low on his narrow hips, and her dress was unbuttoned to the waist. His lids were heavy, his dark eyes hazed, and tension knotted his muscles, giving him a deliciously aroused aura. She sensed that hers was the same.

Deliberately she undid the remaining buttons on her dress, shrugged and let it slide off her shoulders. She pulled his shirt off next, ruffling his hair, then gave his trousers the nudge they needed to fall to the floor. He kicked them aside and stood there in nothing but boxers, tented over his erection, his muscles long and lean and taut, his skin practically quivering with need.

The room darkened as the approaching storm blocked out the sun. The breeze was cool, stirred by the ceiling fan, and the air was heavy and close with anticipation. It crawled along her skin and made her hands unsteady as she opened the front clasp of her bra, then slid it loose, as she guided her beribboned cotton panties over her hips and let them fall.

His gaze dropped from hers, skimming over her body, leaving tingling in its wake, and he swallowed convulsively. His features were sharp, his control nearly gone, but he didn't reach for her.

"It's not too late," she said. "You can walk away." But, of course, he couldn't, not today. Someday, he would. He would finish with her, and in a few months, maybe a year, he would fall in love with a woman of his own social class, his own race, and they would marry and have children and live a conventional wealthy, white Southerner life. But first, for at least a time—a few weeks, a few days or maybe just this hour or two—he would be Anamaria's.

He swallowed again, and a shudder rippled along his muscles, then he stripped off his boxers. "The only walking I intend to do is to that bed. I've waited too long…"

Less than seventy-two hours. Though *her* seventy-two hours had really been a lifetime. Destiny.

She crossed to the nightstand, to the few items she'd unpacked there when she'd arrived, and pulled out a box of condoms. Her grandmothers and aunties taught their girls to be prepared, but it rarely seemed to matter. Duquesne women used every kind of birth control known to man and still conceived. *When it's time, it's time.* Powers greater than pharmaceuticals and barriers decreed when a Duquesne should be born. Still, telling Robbie now that condoms were no likelier to prevent pregnancy in her than the impending rain didn't seem a good idea.

As she tore open the box, he moved to stand close behind her, his hands settling on her shoulders like feathers drifting onto grass. His fingers squeezed lightly, a gentle massage, and she closed her eyes, head tilted to one side, a soft satisfied groan escaping her.

He slid one arm around her middle, pulled her snug against him, and brought his mouth to her ear. "Concentrate, Anamaria. Open the box. Take out a condom. Give it to me so I can…"

The obscenity he whispered would have annoyed her any other time or from any other man, but at that moment, with its hard letters and soft sounds and its inherent naughtiness, it couldn't have seemed more appropriate.

She ripped the box open and showered a dozen plastic-wrapped condoms on the night table. Robbie picked up one, but she caught his hand, prying his fingers open. "Mine."

With her free hand, she pushed him back onto the bed, kneeling on the mattress beside him. He looked amazing, sprawled out, as relaxed as a breathtakingly aroused man could be. His arms and legs were long, muscular, powerful—impressive for a man whose idea of time well spent was in a fishing boat. Dark hair curled lightly across his chest, thickening as it moved down his body, and his arousal…

She smiled as she tore open the plastic and removed the

latex inside. The plastic fluttered to the floor as she unrolled the condom over his erection, taking her time, stroking, petting, making him groan. Protection in place and sweat beading on his forehead, she knelt over him, taking him inside her, sliding slowly enough to make herself groan, to bring her own beads of sweat.

And then he was completely inside her, filling her, stretching her, completing her. Fate, destiny, broken heart—none of it mattered. Only one word came to her dazed mind.

Mine.

The storm came not long after they did, bringing cooler air and rain that fell in a deluge. Thunder shook the old house as lightning flashed through its windows, one moment revealing, the next throwing shadows. When the rain blew in through the west-facing windows, Robbie got up to close them, and the temperature immediately began to climb again.

When he returned to the bedroom, Anamaria was standing at one of the side windows that remained open, a sheet carelessly wrapped around her. It looped low in back, showing the long, elegant line of her spine and the beginning curve of her hip, and in front it revealed more of her breasts than it covered.

She was beautiful. Flawless. She looked like some sort of wanton African Greek goddess, her skin smooth and soft, her body perfect, her features erotic in their exoticness. There was an air of innocence about her, despite the tousled hair, the sweat drying on her skin and the wicked little smile that curved her mouth. Looking at her, he could see the sweet little girl from the picture, standing outside the church, wearing a gap-toothed grin and a pretty pink dress.

But it was the woman that little girl had become that made his mouth go dry and brought his erection back to life.

The woman he still couldn't imagine in the everyday routine of his life.

She didn't glance his way or give any sign that she knew he'd returned. "Mama and I liked the rain when I was little, but when it came down like this, so hard you can't see ten feet, I always thought we would wash away into the river. And when it rained at night, I slept in Mama's bed so that if we did wash away, at least we would wash away together."

A look came across her face—surprise, confusion, sorrow. *I don't remember much about living here,* she'd told him. Now she could add one more memory to the list. How many times had she feared they would wash away before her baby sister actually did? Had she felt guilty? Had she feared that, because she'd thought it, she'd caused it?

No wonder she'd locked away the past.

He went to her, wrapping his arms around her. Her skin was chilled and damp; so was the sheet. He pulled it more snugly around her, then shared his own heat with her. For a time she rested her head on his shoulder, flinching only slightly when the thunder and lightning came. The rain beat down the grass, and streams poured across the yard to empty into the ditches out front. The air outside was sweet and wet, and inside it was warm and smelled of cookies and perfume and sex.

Pretty damn good sex. Best he'd had in...

His jaw tightened. Better not to finish that thought. The best sex ever should mean something; it should be with a woman who was part of his life, not just for a week or two, but forever. The best sex ever should have something to do with love and commitment and belonging together, the two halves of a whole.

"You're thinking too much."

He realized that she'd turned her head to study him and wondered what she'd seen. That he was regretting that she wasn't the woman he wanted? That he wasn't the man she needed? He wanted someone who would meet all the expectations people would have of a woman in his life. She needed someone who didn't give a damn about anyone's expectations except their own. He wanted someone who cared about reputation, status and fitting in, and she needed someone who wanted only to fit into her life.

He wanted a different woman. She deserved a better man.

He swallowed a sigh and rested his chin against her hair. "Thinking too much. That's something no one's ever accused me of."

"You're the irresponsible one."

"The shallow one," he agreed. "The superficial one."

"The one who cares about appearances."

He did. He wasn't proud of it, but he'd never denied it. Maybe it was some flaw inherent in him. Maybe it was because neither Rick nor Russ had ever cared what anyone besides their closest family and friends thought. Maybe Granddad and Grandmother and the snootiest of his relatives had influenced him too much, but he did care.

But in that selective we-are-special Calloway way. It had never mattered if everyone in town knew he'd drunk too much. It hadn't meant a thing that they all knew he'd been reckless and wild and thought himself above the law for more years than youth could explain. It didn't mean a damn thing if they knew he dated the wrong women. Dating was insignificant.

A serious relationship, marriage, children...those were damned significant. Those required the right woman.

He was shallow. Superficial. And a first-class bastard.

When his silence drew out, Anamaria's muscles tensed, then relaxed again. She raised one hand to curve her fingers gently around his wrist. "Don't worry. We Duquesne women are very good at keeping secrets."

Her tone was calm, level, and it angered him. She shouldn't
be so accepting. She should kick his ass out the door—should
have done that instead of touching him. But she didn't, and
he was damned grateful because he didn't know if he could
stay away.

Lightning struck nearby, the crack deafening, and the fan
overhead whirred to a slow stop. Without electricity, the house
went quiet except for the sounds of their breathing, hers
settled, his harder to come by. His chest was tight, and so was
his gut. He would give this month's income for a cold beer
or, better still, a shot of whiskey.

He might give his soul for two shots.

With her free hand, Anamaria traced the caulking that held
the new windowpane in place. "Why would someone throw
bricks through my windows?"

"Kids looking for fun."

She gave him a wry look. "You call that fun?"

"When you're young and stupid…." He shrugged. "You
don't think it was random?"

"No. It's just a feeling… I know, you don't believe in
mumbo jumbo."

No, but he believed in instinct and intuition, and he damn
sure believed in stalkers. They'd almost lost Russ and Jamie
to one the year before. "Why would someone target you?"

"Because of the questions I'm asking about my mother."

"Her death was an accident, so there's nothing to hide
there. You think one of her boyfriends doesn't want to be
outed all these years later? Maybe the baby's father?"

"Charlotte," she murmured. "That was her name."

Glory's affairs and her baby's life had ended more than two
decades ago. Could it possibly matter now to Charlotte's
father if Anamaria discovered his identity? Robbie would like
to think no, certainly not enough to resort to threats, but he

knew better. If the man was married, if he was prominent, if he had family, yes, he might want his indiscretions to stay in the past. After all, Glory and Charlotte were dead. There was no payoff to his secret coming out now, just consequences.

And most people preferred to avoid consequences.

"It will be impossible to prove who fathered Charlotte," he pointed out. "Your mother kept his identity secret, and there's no DNA for comparison. Unless he's willing to talk…." And if he was behind the bricks through the windows, that wasn't likely.

She watched the rain, her expression distant. Her voice was distant, too, when she spoke. "People talked about Mama— women, mostly. They said she was easy, a tramp, a whore. They looked down on her for having us kids without a husband, and they looked down on her even more for letting Lillie and Jass live with their fathers. They said she was a bad mother."

Her smile curled to life like a flower unfurling to the sun. "They couldn't have been more wrong. She was funny and happy, and she loved everything. She played with me and sang songs and told me stories about all the Duquesnes who had already passed."

"Do you remember any of the songs and stories?" Robbie asked quietly.

"I do." Then the smile faded. "But Mama Odette and Auntie Lueena and Auntie Charise sang the same songs and told the same stories. I don't know if my memories are of Mama or them."

"Does it matter?"

Surprise raised her delicately arched brows. "How can it not matter?"

Gathering a handful of trailing sheet, he began maneuvering her backward to the bed. "The songs and stories are the same. You know Glory shared them with you. Does it matter if you remember them in her voice when, in fact, it might have been your grandmother's or your aunt's?" He nudged her onto her back, then unwrapped the sheet as if opening a holiday gift. But no Christmas present in thirty-two years could compare to the sight of Anamaria, naked and beautiful on her white cotton, lace and embroidered bed.

"I don't know," she said, her voice suddenly breathy as he nuzzled her breast. "When you look back on this afternoon someday, will it matter if I'm in the picture, or will any woman do as well? After all, it's the same act. You'll know you had sex with me. Will it matter if you picture some pretty blue-eyed blonde in my place instead?"

Guilt twitched in his gut and between his shoulder blades, but he shoved it away, concentrating instead on her nipple, ripe and swollen and eager for his kiss. When he took it between his teeth, her breath caught, and when he sucked it hard, her fingers laced through his hair, holding his head.

He supported himself on one arm and slid his free hand over her rib cage, satiny skin stretched taut over bone, down to her belly, between her thighs. She opened to him, accepting his fingers, giving a soft keening cry as he slid first one, then another, inside her, as his thumb massaged that small nub of flesh.

He brought her to orgasm, grabbed a condom and did it again, reaching his own orgasm just when he thought the need would kill him. Need. Not wanting. When the shudders eased, he sank down to lie against her, his slick skin pressed to hers, his cheek resting on her shoulder. His heart pounded, and his muscles quivered, sending an occasional spasm through his entire body.

She held him, stroking him, her touches soothing now, comforting. And after a time, after he'd begun to recover, she spoke once again in that calm, accepting voice. "You can replace me in your memories with all the blue-eyed blondes you want. I don't expect anything more than this from you."

Robbie stiffened, but he didn't reply. Maybe that was the problem: no one expected anything from him. No one counted on him, no one relied on him, no one believed he was capable of stepping up, accepting responsibility, being a man.

He didn't even believe it himself.

But damned if he didn't wish Anamaria did.

Chapter 6

The power was back on, the rain still fell and Anamaria sat at the kitchen table, wearing a white nightgown of cotton batiste. The hem bore a ruffle that tickled her knees, and two more served as sleeves on the thin shift. Her feet were drawn up in the chair, one knee bent, her hands clasped around it.

It was nearly seven o'clock, the sky darker than usual because of the rain. She gazed out the window, wondering who had thrown the bricks that afternoon, why they'd done it, if they were out there tonight in the woods, watching.

The shiver that danced down her spine was almost enough to make her close the blinds.

Across from her, Robbie was finishing the last of his dinner. She'd fried red potatoes, onions and peppers, added chopped ham and cheese and topped it off with fried eggs. The fragrant aroma would last far longer than the food.

She'd put on the gown when hunger had driven them from

bed, but he'd gotten dressed, down to his shoes. His clothes hadn't even wrinkled in their hours on the floor; still, they couldn't disguise the fact that he'd been well and truly made love to that afternoon.

So had she. And for the first time in her life, she understood what her family had meant by the Duquesne passion. What had happened in her bedroom hadn't been just sex. She'd been experiencing that since she was sixteen and had enjoyed it, more with some than others.

No, this had been Robbie. She might be interchangeable with other women for him, but he had his own inviolate place in her life. He had taken away her breath and left her a different woman.

Underneath the table, her hand drifted to her stomach. He might have made a mother of her. She had no special gift to tell, though Auntie Charise did. One look, and she would know.

Anamaria preferred to find out the old-fashioned way. She would be back in Savannah by the time her next period was due. Robbie would be sleeping with another woman, and when he thought of her—if he thought of her—it would be as his dirty little secret.

She closed her eyes. She was strong. She was a Duquesne, destined to love well and unwisely, to never marry and to have beautiful daughters. Robbie was so handsome that any daughter of his would be beautiful.

"Anamaria."

She looked at him and found him looking back, his expression troubled. He knew he was going to break her heart, and he regretted it. She didn't. Oh, sure, she wished things could be different, but she would never regret this affair.

"What you said earlier—"

She knew exactly what he was talking about: replacing her in his memories. Unwilling to discuss it now, she slid her feet to the floor, rose and carried their dishes to the sink. While her back was turned, she managed a credible smile, then faced him. "What happens in my bedroom stays in my bedroom."

He opened his mouth as if he might argue, then closed it again. He found it easy to not pursue difficult conversations. It was one of the benefits of privilege, she supposed, or of being the youngest child, the favored grandchild, the handsome, sexy, charming sweet-talker.

After rinsing the dishes, she returned to the table. "Do you have plans for this evening?" A date, work, clubbing with his friends, Thursday-night poker with his buddies—she didn't know how he usually spent his time. Selfishly, at the moment all she cared about was his time with her.

He shook his head. "Do you have something in mind?"

She sat across from him, taking in his dark gaze, his expression that managed both satisfaction and discomfort, the stubble of beard that would give him a disreputable look if he wasn't one of *the* Calloways. She thought about the things they could do. Sex. Sex. And more sex.

But instead she said, "I'd like to go to the place where my mother's body was found."

Automatically he looked out the window. "It's dark and raining."

"It was dark and raining that night, too."

"You won't be able to see much."

"I don't want to see. I want to feel." Her hands trembled, and she moved them to her lap. It might be crazy. Traipsing around in the dark and rain in an unfamiliar place—okay, so there was no *might* about it. But the idea had taken root, and she didn't want to shake it. The weather was right, and so was the time. If those conditions might help open her to whatever spiritual residue remained at the river, she would take advantage of them.

If he would go with her.

He wasn't the type for mucking around in the nighttime rain, and he certainly wasn't dressed for it tonight, but after a moment and another long look outside, he nodded. "Sure. Why not?"

Before he could change his mind, she surged from the chair and went into the bedroom, changing into jeans, a T-shirt and running shoes, pulling a slicker from the closet. She stuffed her keys into her pocket and returned to the kitchen to find him standing in the doorway.

"It'll be easier to reach it from the park, and I can stop at my place and change on the way."

He was suggesting that they go separately. He didn't want to be seen leaving the neighborhood with her, didn't want her seen at his condo. She tamped down the disappointment that rose. "Okay. I'll meet you at the park—"

Or maybe that wasn't what he'd meant at all. Before she could finish, he grabbed her hand, turned and pulled her down the hall and out the door. He stopped on the porch long enough for her to lock up, then ran with her down the steps and through puddles to his car.

The torrential rain had passed, leaving behind a steady fall of the sort that could last for days. It overflowed the ditches and collected in the streets, reflecting headlights and street-lamps, and it fled the windshield wipers in undulating drops. She listened to the rhythmic swipe of the blades and the softer, also rhythmic tenor of his breathing before breaking the silence. "What do you normally do on Thursday nights?"

He shrugged. "Watch TV. Play poker with Tommy and a few guys. Nothing special. What about you?"

"Thursdays are my late night at the shop. I'm there until nine, and I have to be at the diner at six the next morning, so I go home and to bed."

"What kind of shop?"

"Mama Odette's place." She smiled. "Did you think I set up a card table and two folding chairs on a street corner?"

"I thought you probably worked out of your house."

With a sign that said "Sister Anamaria Sees All," she recalled from their first meeting. "A lot of readers do. I don't want strangers coming into my house, and Mama Odette's shop is just a few blocks from both the diner and the house. It's convenient."

"You have regular clients?"

"I do. Just like you. Though I'm fairly sure my advice comes quite a bit cheaper than yours."

He smiled faintly as he turned off Carolina Avenue just before the bridge that crossed the river, followed the street for a few moments, then turned into a gated community nestled along the river. An elaborate brick-and-iron sign identified it as River Crossing, a dozen or so buildings housing five units each. The houses looked a century old in the soft light from the streetlamps, but the only ancient feeling to the place came from the land itself.

Robbie's condo was in the best location, on the south end of a building that faced the river. With red brick and white columns, decorative iron and a wicker-decorated porch, it was gracious and lovely. He parked at the curb—the garages were at the rear of the building—and shut off the engine. "It'll just take— Do you want to come in?"

Of course she did. She wanted to see where he ate, slept and entertained the other women in his life. But because she didn't know whether the invitation was sincere or merely manners kicked into gear by some emotion that had crossed her face, she shook her head. "I'll wait."

Her answer relieved him. No pesky explanations to offer to nosy neighbors. He got out of the car and jogged to the door.

As rain gathered to obscure her view, she called up an image of her Savannah neighborhood: a few square miles crisscrossed by railroad tracks, the houses aged, the businesses shabby. She lived in a duplex, carved out of a house that was small to start with. It was drafty in winter, and with a window air conditioner that made the heat bearable, it was noisy in summer. The furniture was secondhand, the appliances thirdhand. All totaled, her every possession, including her car, didn't equal even a fraction of what this condo must be worth.

But she didn't envy Robbie's wealth. She was happy in Savannah. Everything she needed was within walking distance—both of her jobs, the market, their church, her grandmother, aunts and cousins. Sometimes Duquesne women had a lot of money, like Lucia with the wooden chest filled with jewels; most of the time they didn't. But they always had enough. Enough money, enough family, enough love.

Robbie certainly had the money and the family. Did he have enough love?

He came out again, wearing jeans, a slicker like hers and hiking boots that had seen better days. In one hand, he carried two bright yellow lanterns.

It took only a few minutes to reach Gullah Park. The lot was deserted and dark, the lights unable to penetrate the thick leaves of the trees under which they parked. He handed her a lantern but didn't let go once she'd taken it. "Are you sure about this?"

"I am." Some part of her was even looking forward to it. Another part knew she couldn't do it without him at her side.

The rain merely dripped on them until they cleared the trees and reached the trail. She didn't bother to pull the slicker's hood up; she liked the rain, cool and gentle, on her face.

They walked in silence. She could think of a hundred things to say—questions to ask, secrets to share—but it seemed wrong, indulging in casual conversation on this particular journey. When they reached the bleached remnants of an old dock, Robbie silently tucked her hand into his. They'd left the park path behind and were following a dirt trail so hard-packed that the afternoon's heavy rain hadn't marked it. There was no traffic on the river, no sounds at all besides the rain and their breathing and the steadily increasing beat of her heart.

A few yards beyond the old dock, she stopped. Her fingers were knotted around his, and her stomach was knotted as well. With some effort, she turned off the flashlight, loosed her fingers and took a few steps alone.

This was the place.

Slowly she turned in a circle. The trail, pounded out at the top of the riverbank. Trees, tall spindly shadows of loblolly pines, the heavier growth of oaks and gums. Shrubs, deadwood, the deep, dark curves of the river. This was the last place her mother had been. The last things she'd seen, smelled, touched. The last thoughts she'd had—for her babies, her mama, her sisters and nieces, her hopes and regrets, her sorrows and her joy—had dissipated into the air here. The place she'd given birth. The place she'd died.

Anamaria breathed deeply, smelling rain and mud and pines and...almonds. She inhaled again, the scent remaining strong, sweet, and sparking a sweeter memory. "We baked almond-meringue cookies that afternoon," she said, her voice little more than a whisper as she welcomed back the time. "It was my job to put one nut on each cookie, but I ran out of them with two trays of cookies left. *You're eating all the almonds,* she scolded, but she laughed when she said it, and then she took another bag from the cabinet, and we finished the cookies and ate the rest together."

A warm tear trickled down her wet skin. Bending, she set the lantern on the ground, then carefully made her way down the slope toward the river. It was muddy at the bottom, sucking at her shoes as she moved to the fallen tree that extended out into the water. Leaning against it for support, she stared at the place where her mother had died.

"I asked her not to go out that evening. I could tell it was going to rain, and my stomach hurt really bad and I didn't know why and it scared me. But Mama said I'd just eaten too many cookies, and she made me some ginger tea. She said she had to go, that she had appointments to keep, and she tucked me under a quilt on the couch, kissed me, wrapped her shawl around her and left as soon as Marguerite came."

She stared a long time at the image that had evaded her for so many years: Mama, her hair loose and curling, her eyes bright, her smile reassuring. Her dress was blue and white and stretched tightly across her belly, and her shawl was faded and soft, pieced together by Mama Odette from old velvets and wools belonging to one passed-on Duquesne or another. It was long, rectangular, and Mama had worn it everywhere.

Her brow wrinkled. Where was it now?

"But it wasn't too many cookies." Robbie switched off his own light and let his eyes adjust to the darkness. Despite the slicker, he was wet pretty much everywhere, with rain trickling down his face and scalp and soaking into his shirt. Anamaria was wet, too, but she didn't seem to notice. She leaned against the oak tree, fingers pressing hard against the smooth surface where the bark had long ago peeled away. Her eyes were closed, the sorrow etched on her face.

"Why was she here? Where had she been? Why did she leave her car and walk all this way? She loved the rain, she loved the night, but she was nine months' pregnant. Why did she come here?"

He set his lantern next to hers and followed her trail down the slope. When he reached her, he slid his arms around her and tried to pull her close, but she stood rigid. "I don't know, Anamaria. No one knows."

"*She* knows! She knows, but she won't tell, just like she wouldn't tell who Charlotte's father was."

"Anamaria… Annie, she's *dead*."

She jerked away from him, took a few steps, then sank into a crouch in the mud, hugging herself tightly. "What were you doing here?" she whispered. "Why didn't you listen to me? What good is knowing something's going to happen if nobody listens?"

Guilt sharpened her voice and stabbed through him, too. She'd tried, in her five-year-old fashion, to tell her mother, but Glory had failed to recognize her daughter's actions for the warning they were. She'd died as a result, along with the baby, and Anamaria had blocked those memories from her mind.

For the warning they were. God, was he starting to buy into this? Did he really believe that Anamaria's stomach-ache and fears had been a sign of impending doom that the little girl hadn't known how to read? That she'd known Glory was in danger, that she'd really seen a vision of her mother's death?

A couple of days ago, it would have been easier to shrug off. Tonight, in this place…

Boots squishing, he crouched behind her and wrapped his arms around her, refusing to let her maintain any distance this time. After a moment, she raised both hands to grip his arms, holding on tightly enough to hurt.

"You don't feel her, do you?" She didn't wait for him to answer. "I do. I feel her…essence. Her memory. The part of her that was left behind when she passed. It still lingers."

"Like her soul?" He felt foolish asking. He'd never given thought to souls or essences, to what happened when a body died. All he'd known were the consequences for those left behind. His father had died; life had been better. Granddad had died; life had been poorer.

"Not her soul. That's passed on. Her imprint. A person can't die, a life can't end, without leaving some mark, some sign that she was there."

"And you sense these marks?" Another foolish question. His brothers would laugh at him. His mother would worry about him. Tommy…maybe not so much. After all, his great-grandma Rosa had been a believer.

She shook her head, water spraying from her hair. "Sensing the imprint of everyone who's ever passed on could drive a person crazy. But this is my *mother.* She lay here. She died here. She took her last breath here. She left this life right here where we are."

There was no doubt of that, Robbie thought, gazing at the water where it lapped against the shore. The fisherman had found Glory; the police had documented her death. But was Anamaria really feeling something, or was she *imprinting* what she knew of her mother's death with guesses and guilt?

"She gave life, too," he reminded her. "Charlotte was born right here. She died, if not here, then very nearby. What about her? What do you feel about her?" It had been February when Glory and the baby had died. The medical examiner had estimated survival for a newborn infant whose birth was unattended in such conditions at mere minutes.

Anamaria stilled, her breathing growing slow and steady. Her eyes closed, she looked as if she might have been asleep, and for an instant, the photograph of Glory from the police file flashed into his mind. She had looked asleep, too, except for the gash on her forehead.

Anamaria opened her eyes again. "I don't feel her— Charlotte. I don't feel anything at all. No imprint, no memory, nothing."

"You said you don't usually see things about people close to you."

"I don't see futures, but I saw our mother's death. Why can't I tell anything about Charlotte's?"

"Maybe they were wrong. Maybe she didn't die here." With a lot of rain, the river current would have been swifter than usual. Maybe it had carried the baby beyond the range of sensing.

He shook his head. He was cold and wet, and the muscles in his thighs were starting to cramp, yet there he sat having a conversation about visions of death and spiritual imprints as if they were rational things.

He eased to his feet, taking her with him. "Let's go back to the car."

She nodded, but when he started up the hill, she remained where she was, staring at the river. He retraced his steps, took her hand and pulled her up the slope. On the path he retrieved their lanterns, switched his on and headed back toward the paved trail, keeping her chilled fingers wrapped in his.

They were halfway there when she stopped abruptly, dragging him to a halt, as well. "Maybe she's not dead."

He gazed at her, but when he opened his mouth to speak, she laid her free hand across it to silence him.

"They never found her body. They never found anything. Mama Odette knows people's fates, *especially* people close to her, but she doesn't know Charlotte's. And Mama doesn't know, either. Maybe they don't know because Charlotte isn't dead."

He pushed her hand away, then gripped it as tightly as he held the other. "Then where is she?"

Anamaria didn't answer. She wanted to—he could see it in her eyes—but there was nothing to say. The baby was dead. Her first breath had been damn near her last. And Glory and Mama Odette didn't know because people didn't *know* that sort of thing. It was all part of the scam the family had been running for generations.

Her lips compressed, her brows furrowed, as anxiety, need and hope crossed her features. For an instant, the hope faded, then returned just as fiercely. "What about the shawl? Where is it?"

Glory had wrapped her shawl around her before leaving, Anamaria had said. "Your grandmother's probably packed it away somewhere."

She shook her head. "That shawl was special. Mama Odette made it, and Mama never went anywhere without it. She wore it when she was chilled or wrapped it around me when I was cold. We had picnics on it. She covered me with it when I fell asleep in church. There was a piece of fabric in it from every Duquesne in the last hundred years. If Mama Odette had it, she would have given it to me."

"Maybe Glory forgot it somewhere."

Again she shook her head solemnly. "You'd be more likely to forget your Vette somewhere."

"Maybe she dropped it in the river." Robbie swiped his hair from his forehead, then brushed back her hair. "I know what you're hoping, Annie—that someone came along, that they found Charlotte, took the shawl and wrapped her in it and that she's safe, alive and well somewhere. But look around. What are the odds that someone happened along on a night like this? You're not going to have any fishermen, no hunters, no joggers, no hikers. No one came along. No one took Charlotte. No one saved her."

A breath shuddered through her, and for a moment he thought she might cry. Instead, she raised her chin, stiffened her spine and fixed a determined look on him. "My sister did not die back there."

He stiffened his spine, too, and used the harsh, confronting tone that stood him well in courtroom cross-examinations. "Where she died doesn't matter. All that matters is that she did die."

"If the police were wrong about where, they could be wrong about how. They could be wrong about *whether*."

"Why don't you call them?" he demanded as she pulled her hand free, crossed her arms over her middle and started along the path. "Tell them your mother lost an old handmade shawl that night and that you can't feel her dead baby's *imprint* on the riverbank. I bet they'll want to open an investigation immediately."

"Maybe I'll do that. Tommy Maricci is a conscientious detective, and he's got believer's blood flowing through his veins." She tossed her hair over one shoulder. "On top of that, he likes me."

Jealousy curled, hot and ugly, in Robbie's gut. "And do you like him?"

"I do." With that blunt response, she strode ahead. He stood looking after her, wondering what the hell he was doing. He could be at home, warm and dry, kicked back in front of the television. Packing his car and heading off for a long weekend at his uncle Travis's beach house on Kiawah Island. Driving west to Atlanta for a few days of easy relaxation and easier sex with an ex-girlfriend he still saw on occasion.

But, no, he was soaked to the skin, cold, frustrated, jealous of his own best buddy over a woman who was as ill-suited to his life as he was to hers, and worried about her. Worried she would convince herself that Charlotte was alive. Worried about the disappointment when she had to accept—again—that it wasn't true. Worried about the guilt she felt. That the memories she'd unlocked tonight might have been better forgotten.

He worried that someone had vandalized her house, whether the act had been random or deliberate. That she might get hurt.

That he might hurt her. That she might hurt him. That he would disappoint her as he had always disappointed everyone.

Damn, Harrison Kennedy wasn't paying him nearly enough for this case.

By the time he caught up with Anamaria, she was waiting at the car, her defensive posture relaxed. "Her father," she said as he drew near. "Charlotte's father could have taken her. Glory had two appointments that evening. One was Lydia, but no one knew who the second was, just that it wasn't any of her regular clients. Maybe it was Charlotte's father. The baby was due in a few days. Maybe he needed assurance that she wasn't going to tell anyone his name. Maybe she needed money for the medical bills. Maybe that was why she was out along the river, where no one could possibly see them together. And she went into labor and he couldn't help her, but he took the baby. His baby."

"*If* you're right…" He clenched his jaw. It was believable: a man with a pregnant mistress, a single mother who wasn't looking for marriage but needed money, an out-of-the-way meeting place. But if the man had needed reassurance from Glory, if he'd taken the baby but left her, then it became very possible that Glory's death hadn't been accidental at all. She hadn't just *gone* into labor, according to the autopsy; she'd fallen and hit her head, and the trauma had precipitated labor.

Instead of falling, maybe she'd been shoved. Or maybe the blow to the head had come first. Maybe Charlotte's father had assured her silence by killing her.

What kind of bastard killed the woman carrying his own child?

One with a lot to lose. Even twenty-three years later.

Anamaria had a lot to lose, as well, if that was the case.

He opened the car door and waited for her to settle inside, then circled to the driver's side. He didn't speak on the way back to her house, and neither did she. When he pulled into the driveway and shifted into Park, she turned as if to say good-night, but the words faded unspoken as he shut off the engine and got out. He wasn't leaving her alone. Not yet.

They left their slickers, shoes and socks on the porch. She unlocked the door, stopped a few feet inside, then gave a soft sigh. "It's all right."

He checked anyway, making sure each window was locked and intact and that the back door was locked, as well. When he finished, he found her in the bathroom, stripped of her wet clothes, wrapped in a bath towel and blotting water from her hair with another towel. Arousal stirred in his groin, along with something else. Something unfamiliar, possessive... tender. Something that knotted in his chest, aching even when he absentmindedly rubbed it.

She smiled at his reflection in the mirror, a subdued, tired gesture. "Thank you for going with me."

He managed a *you're welcome* as the phone rang in the kitchen. Her gaze flickered that way, but she made no move from the sink. "Will you get that for me?"

"Sure." He padded down the hall and into the kitchen, grabbing the phone on the third ring. "Hello."

There was a moment's silence, and immediately he thought about the person who'd sneaked out of the woods that afternoon to give Anamaria a malicious welcome-home. The hairs on his arms stood on end, and he was reaching for the cell phone in his pocket to call Tommy when the caller finally spoke.

"Well. Here I am on my deathbed, picturing my grandbaby just worrying herself sick about me, and instead she's entertaining a gentleman and not giving me any thought at all. Isn't that a fine situation?"

Mama Odette's voice was similar to Anamaria's, but the

cadence of her speech was slow, befitting a Georgia woman born and bred, and her accent was heavy as honey.

"I doubt you're on your deathbed, Miz Duquesne, and I'm no gentleman at all."

She laughed, a rich rumble. "Then what kind of man are you, Robert Calloway?"

"The kind you probably warned Anamaria about."

"The best kind." She laughed again, but underneath it he heard the whoosh of hospital equipment.

"No one's called me Robert in twenty-five years."

"No one's called me Miz Duquesne in about that long. If you're not comfortable with the Mama part, you can just call me Odette."

"And you can call me Robbie."

From down the hall came the sound of bathwater running. He thought of Anamaria, naked, sliding into a tub smelling of jasmine and piled high with bubbles, and his body responded, albeit accompanied by guilt, since he was on the phone with the grandmother who'd raised her. Swallowing hard, he shut off the overhead light, leaving only the bulb over the sink burning, and stretched the phone cord so he could sit at the table.

"Anamaria's told you about me."

"Not so much. I see more than I hear."

"Yeah, that's right. You're a psychic, too."

"And you're a skeptic. But that's all right. Everyone learns eventually. 'There are more things in heaven and earth,' and all that."

An elderly con artist quoting Shakespeare to him. That was a first.

"Is my girl handy where I can talk at her a minute?"

He gauged the length of the phone cord, figuring it would fall about fifteen feet short of the bathroom. "She, uh…" Well, hell, there was something too damn intimate about his being in the house while her girl took a bath. Even the most naive of parents would make the leap to the fact that they were sleeping together, and Odette, based on all he'd heard, wasn't naive.

Once again she laughed, a sound that obviously came easily to her. "Now I *know* I didn't interrupt you in the act, because you're not all out of breath, and I don't hear Anamaria at all. It's perfectly all right for you to say, 'She's soaking in the tub.' I'm way down here in Savannah, and in a hospital bed to boot, so it's not like I'm gonna come looking for you with my shotgun. Besides, she's a grown woman now. She chooses who she chooses."

His face flushed hot. He was a skeptic and a coward and a pain in the ass, but he was circumspect about sex. If the women he was involved with chose to share, fine, but he usually kept his mouth shut. It was probably the only thing he had in common with his old man. Gerald had been so expert at hiding his affairs that Sara's first clue had come after his death, when she'd discovered nine-year-old Mitch.

Had Charlotte's father been as expert?

"How's my girl doin'?" Odette asked, then went on before he could answer. "I hated to ask her to go there and take care of my business for me, but these doctors won't let me out of here. They keep telling me I'm gonna die. Well, heavens, chile, we're *all* gonna die. It's just a matter of when. I just couldn't go, though, without knowing more about my baby's last days. I had twenty-three years of good health to find out, but…"

All the pleasure faded from her voice. "It was such a hard time for all of us, but especially Anamaria. Oh, she loved her mama. You never seen a mama and baby as happy as them. When she come here to live with me, it was like all the light had gone out of her. She fretted for her mama and for that baby sister she never got to know, and then she just put it all out of her mind. Did such a good job of forgetting that when she wanted to remember, she couldn't recall a thing."

He thought of her, recent moments flashing through his mind. "She's all right. She's strong."

"Oh, chile, Duquesne women has always had to be strong. We don't have the kind of life that other women have, but God gives us strength enough to handle it. How about you? How strong are you?"

His head aching, he squeezed his eyes shut tight. "Not enough."

"I don't know. You know right from wrong, even if you don't always do it. I bet you were a wild one when you was a boy. Probably gave your mama every gray hair she's got, you and your brothers. And that's okay. That's how boys should be. But you know what? When the time comes, you'll do what you have to."

There was a pause, another voice in the background. *Time for your medication, Mama Odette.* Then she turned her attention back to him. "Tell my girl I called and I love her and she's all right. And you—you watch out for her, too. You'll do that."

It wasn't a question, but he answered it anyway. "Yeah, I'll do it."

She chuckled. "Good night, Robbie Calloway. You know, there's more to you than you think."

He waited until the line went dead, then slowly hung up. *You'll do what you have to.* A lot of faith from someone who clearly didn't know him. Outside of his office, he didn't live up to obligations; he didn't accept burdens. He was the irresponsible one.

Besides, he didn't have a clue what it was he needed to do. Stay with Anamaria?

Or walk away?

Chapter 7

She was all right.

Robbie had passed on the message from Mama Odette, and in the early dawn hours the following day, Anamaria knew it was true. Mama Odette had read her cards, spoken to her spirit guides, all topped off with a generous dose of good ol' prayer, and the answers were the same. Anamaria was all right.

Did you ask Auntie Charise what she saw? she'd wanted to know. But by the time she'd finished her bath, and Robbie had carried her to bed and made love to her until she was senseless, it had been too late for calling her family. She didn't need Charise's confirmation anyway. Things were different. She'd awakened a few minutes ago to the certainty that her life had changed for good. She had found passion, and her own sweet little girl was now growing safe and protected inside her.

Unwise love and a pretty daughter to remind her of it. That was her destiny, and she accepted it, but was it wrong to want more? To wish that just once destiny could include a husband, marriage and a little convention? To wish that her daughter might always know the love and acceptance of her father and his family?

Lillie and Jass both had that, but they'd had to leave the Duquesne family to get it. They'd been sent away and raised to fit in someplace else so thoroughly that they no longer fit in where they came from. They didn't know Mama Odette the way they should; they didn't know the family history, didn't understand the family gifts, didn't develop their own gifts. They were Duquesnes only by birth, not by living.

Anamaria couldn't bear that for her child.

Behind her Robbie stirred, one arm pillowing his head, one leg thrust out from beneath the sheet. She hadn't asked him to stay last night, though she'd wanted to. She'd watched her aunties and her cousins never ask for a thing from a man beyond money to help raise their children. Mama Odette had been with the same man off and on for twenty years. She never asked him to go when she got tired of him, never asked him to stay when he was leaving. She accepted what he gave her, just as she accepted what he denied her.

Call it a curse, fate or destiny, but sometimes it sucked.

Easing from the bed, she pulled on her nightgown, then walked barefooted through the house. Light shone in wedges across the floor, reminding her of other early mornings, when she and Glory had slipped outside to sit on the back stoop and watch the stars twinkle out in the face of the rising sun. If it was chilly, they'd wrapped the shawl around them both, and if they were feeling silly, they'd run barefooted across the grass, leaving trails in the dew.

It felt so good to have some of those memories back. Foolishly, she'd thought if she'd unlocked one, they would all return, all those years of living in this house with Mama. But she'd been only five years old. She'd lacked the kind of recall adults had. A few memories might be the best a former child could hope for.

After completing her walk through the house, she returned to the bedroom, turned on the tiny frilly lamp on the dresser and took a shirt and capri pants from their hangers. She was about to turn away when her attention caught on the suitcase above. Behind it was the wooden chest, still unopened. *When it's time*, Mama Odette had told her as she handed over the chest.

She gazed at the chest, then at Robbie, now snoring lightly. He would go through it for her, or with her. He would share the task and his strength if she asked him to. But hadn't she just reminded herself that her family didn't ask for things from the men in their lives?

She lifted the box from the shelf, set it on the rug beside the bed, then seated herself cross-legged with the mattress at her back. The filigree latch was stiff from disuse, but it lifted. Her fingers trembled with emotion, but they raised the lid.

She was afraid of what she would find inside, and of what she wouldn't.

The springs creaked; then soft footsteps circled the bed. A moment later Robbie slid down to sit beside her on the floor, his shoulder bumping hers companionably. He was naked and not the least bit uncomfortable with it, or with the silence that cocooned them in the thin circle of light.

Secured to the inside of the lid was a photograph, the edges curled, the colors faded. When she pulled on it, the tape fell away, landing on the rug.

"Sometimes the daddies let Lillie and Jass come for a visit," she said softly, cradling the snapshot where Robbie could see it, too. "That was what we called most of the men—the daddies. There were so many of them, usually far out of our lives. It wasn't worth it to us girls to remember their names."

"That's Augusta. Downtown at the river." He grinned. "You look like a princess."

She grinned, too. She'd been standing on a wall that made her head and shoulders taller than both of her sisters, with her hair in beaded braids and her dress fussy enough for any toddler beauty pageant. "I don't know whether I really liked pink, or if Mama did, but it's what I'm wearing in just about every picture before I turned ten."

Glory was in pink, too, eye-popping bright, and looking as if she didn't have a care in the world. Her arms were around her three girls, and Jass rested her head on Glory's swollen belly. According to the date on the back, it had been taken two months before she died.

"What else is in there?" he asked, but he didn't reach in, instead letting her proceed at her own pace.

"I don't know. Stuff that was in the house, in Mama's purse and her car. Mama Odette's been keeping it for me for years, but I never looked. At first, all I remembered was the vision, and I didn't want to see anything else. Then I couldn't remember. For a long time, I pretended that none of it mattered. I had more family than most people would know what to do with. I was happy. What did it matter that I never knew my father and couldn't remember my mother?"

"Then Mama Odette got sick."

"And it was time. Time for me to remember. To pay my respects to Mama. Someday I'm going to have daughters of my own, and I'm going to tell them all the stories she told me, and I'm going to tell them about her. About how much she loved us. About what a good mother she was, and what a good grandmother she would have been."

The photo trembled when she mentioned having daughters

of her own. In her lifetime, not one Duquesne woman had had two children by the same father. They were a vast family of half sisters. How dearly she would love to be the first one to break that tradition.

Robbie steadied her hand with his own, his fingers firm and warm where hers were shaky and cold. After a moment, she released the photo to him and took out the next item in the chest. A bonnet, sized for an infant, fine white linen edged with lace and tied with pale pink ribbon. More photos: Glory with Lillie's father, with Jass's, with other men neither of them knew in places they didn't recognize. Enclosed in a folded sheet decorated with a crayoned heart were a few dried dandelions, and beneath it, a half-dozen slim spiral notebooks, held together with a rubber band.

She pulled the rubber band, and it broke. Each cover was marked with a name: Savannah, Peach Orchard, Charleston, Beaufort, Atlanta, Copper Lake. Each held names, addresses with directions, phone numbers, dates and times, all in her mother's handwriting, which was as gawky as she had been graceful.

"They're appointment books," Robbie said quietly.

Anamaria selected the one identified as Copper Lake and opened it. The wire binding was warped, and it crackled the pages as she turned them. "Mama Odette uses a calendar from the local funeral home, and I have a date book. Auntie Charise uses a BlackBerry. She does readings by e-mail and text message and has her own Web site. She's woo-woo meets high tech."

His smile came and went as she turned to the last filled pages in the notebook. Glory had shared none of Charise's organizational skills. There were names with no numbers, dates and times with no names. Sometimes she abbreviated names to initials, then a few lines down wrote them out in full.

The final page held two entries: *Liddy, 5:00,* dated February 18, and the other, *2/21* scrawled inside a heart.

"Maybe her second appointment that evening was a date instead," Robbie suggested.

"She was three days from her due date. She was big and round and cumbersome and forbidden from having sex. Not what most men find prime date material."

"You'd still be gorgeous and sexy even if you were about to deliver triplets."

Anamaria stilled on the outside, but everything inside was fluttering—her heart, her breath, the baby girl she was convinced had found life there. Would Robbie be around when their daughter's birth grew near? Probably not. She would send him a polite note from Savannah, once medical tests had confirmed what she already knew, and he could acknowledge it or ignore it as he chose.

She thought he would ignore it. Robbie Calloway admitting to his conservative family, friends and clients that he'd fathered a child with a mixed-race fortune-telling fraud? Ignoring their part-black babies was an age-old tradition for wealthy Southern men. If the Calloways had been typical slaveholders, his distant grandfathers, uncles and cousins had done it a time or two. It would be no stretch for him to.

Though it would break another piece of her heart.

He grew serious again. "How sick is Mama Odette?"

A lump formed in Anamaria's throat, and her vision blurred before she blinked it clear again. "The doctors say she's dying. She says God doesn't share his plans for her with such meddling men. When it's her time, she'll go, but until then she's got a life to live."

"Good attitude."

"Yeah. I'm going to be just like her when I reach her age— gray and round, speaking my mind, surrounded by sisters and daughters and granddaughters and nieces. They'll be sorry to see me go, but they'll be grateful, too, for the life I lived while I was here."

He brushed a strand of hair back, tucking it behind her ear. "Don't those daughters need a father?"

She raised her gaze to find him closer than she'd realized, watching her with such intensity that shivers rippled across her skin. "Duquesne women don't marry," she reminded him softly. "We just fall madly in love, then use our babies to mend our broken hearts."

His fingertip feathered across the curve of her ear. "Is that a law?" he teased. "Can I find it in the Georgia Code?"

Her head tilted, and he continued stroking, along her jaw, the pad of his fingertip bearing a small callus. He had good hands—strong, gentle, unpampered. A woman or an infant could find extraordinary comfort there. "It's worse than a law. It's a curse. The price we pay for being extraordinary women with extraordinary gifts."

He stopped stroking her, and she missed the touch. He didn't move away but shifted so he could better see her, one arm resting on the mattress, his head resting on that hand. "What happens if you get married anyway?"

"What happens?" she echoed.

"Does your groom burst into flames at the altar? Does he get zapped into some parallel universe? Do all those who have passed before descend on him to keep him from getting to the church on time?" He shrugged. "Curses have to have consequences. What are the consequences of this one?"

She stared at him. It was such a simple question, but she'd never asked it before. Oh, she'd asked Mama Odette *why* often enough to drive a lesser woman crazy. *Why aren't you married? Why isn't Auntie Lueena married? Why isn't Auntie*

Charise married? Why do we all have different daddies? Why are there no men in our family?

Because that's the way it is, chile, Mama Odette had answered when Anamaria was younger, but as she got older, the answer had changed. *It's the curse of the Duquesne women.*

"It's not a curse," Robbie said. "It's tradition. Just like it's tradition in my family for all the men to go to law school."

"But your brothers aren't lawyers," she murmured, still caught up in the import of his simple question. *What happens?* In two hundred years no one had bothered to find out. Had it just been circumstance that made her relatives stop marrying? Slavery had been a hard life, and then the war had begun, disrupting their worlds. A lot of women who would have married, raised families and lived normal lives had found themselves following different paths after the war. When had it gone from happenstance to destiny, from coincidence to curse?

"Actually, Russ is. He just chooses not to practice. Rick was the first one to break with tradition, and lightning didn't strike him dead. My grandparents didn't disinherit him. Society didn't shun him. And Mitch wasn't raised as a Calloway, so the family had no expectations for him."

But Robbie *had* been raised a Calloway, and there were a lot of expectations for him. Marrying within his race and class was one of them.

"It's just not done," she said at last.

"But what happens if it is?"

"Nothing happens, because that's just the way it is. There hasn't been a marriage in our family in two hundred years."

"What happened to that one?"

Her laughter was tinged with discomfort. "Two hundred years ago? I don't know." But she did. It was part of the history passed down from one daughter to the next. Etienne and Alfreda Duquesne had raised four daughters—Harriett,

Florence, Ophelia and Gussie. At the age of sixty-one, Etienne had died defending the plantation he'd called home all his life. Two days later Alfreda had passed, too.

And a tradition had begun.

She stared at Robbie a long time before slowly reaching into the chest again.

A cracked wallet, holding a driver's license and Social Security card and stuffed to the breaking point with photographs of daughters and nieces. A tattered storybook that brought tears to Anamaria's eyes. A well-worn deck of tarot cards. A soft velvet bag of crystals and charms. A Bible, its red cover stamped with gold letters in the lower right-hand corner: Glory Duquesne.

A few of my favorite things, Robbie thought, the tune dancing through his head. The important things in a person's life reduced to what would fit inside a wooden chest.

A handful of baby clothes. Some photographs Anamaria identified as being of Odette, Charise and Lueena, along with Odette's mother, Chessie. A mother-of-pearl cross on a sterling chain. Cards marking birthdays, Mother's Day, Christmas. A few dried rose corsages, fragile as dust, the stickpins dull and rusty. Church programs, bits of ribbon, what might have been at one time a lucky penny. And underneath it all, a small stack of memorial pamphlets from funerals, with newspaper obituaries tucked inside.

He read each name as Anamaria sifted through them. None of the services were local; no one sounded familiar.

"This was Mama's father," she said, handing him the last one. "When Mama Odette told him she was pregnant, he said he'd send her to prison on trumped-up charges if she ever contacted him again, so she never did. The first time Mama saw him, he was lying in a casket."

The picture showed a stern white man; the obituary identified him as a retired judge in Savannah, survived by a wife, three children and six grandchildren. Of course, there was no mention of his black daughter and granddaughters.

"Hard to imagine Mama Odette with him."

"Isn't it," Anamaria agreed. Leaning forward, the fabric of her gown pulling tight over her spine and the curve of her butt, she made sure the chest was empty, then sat back. "Well." Her sigh said more than the word. She'd hoped to find something significant inside the box, something that pointed to Glory's lovers, to Charlotte's father.

"We have her client list," he reminded her as he picked up the Copper Lake notebook, flipping through the pages.

A loose piece of paper slipped out, fluttering to the floor between them. It was buff in color, heavyweight, a jagged corner torn from a piece of stationery. The printing on one side showed a lowercase cursive *s* in bold brown ink. By hand on the other side someone had scrawled a note: *Tuesday, 6:30, Lodge.*

Glory had had two appointments the night she died, one at five with Lydia, the other after, and she'd intended to be home by eight-thirty. A six-thirty meeting certainly fit into the time frame.

"I don't know anyone named Lodge," he said before Anamaria could ask.

"Maybe we'll find him in the notebook." She eased to her feet, stretching, then lifted the chest to the bed, laying its contents beside it before she sat down.

Robbie stretched, too, then glanced out the window. It was still dark, the humidity so heavy that it hung in thin clouds just above the ground. They had probably an hour and a half before the sky lightened and the town started stirring. It was an ungodly hour of the morning to be up; he could count on one hand the number of things that could get him out of bed before the sun: fishing, a vacation, sex.

He thought about it a moment, then amended the last: sex with Anamaria.

He eased to his feet and went into the bathroom, where his clothes hung over the shower rod, still damp. The boxers were clammy but went on without a problem; the jeans were clammier and required a lot of effort.

"I need a shower," he remarked when he returned to the bedroom, still tugging at denim that wanted to cling where it shouldn't.

"And a shave," Anamaria said helpfully.

He did have a pretty good bristle-thing going on, which he didn't mind, but it was her delicate skin that suffered for it. "I'll bring breakfast when I come back. What would you like?"

"I can cook." A half-dozen pillows were propped behind her back, and her gown was tugged over her knees, where the baby bonnet rested. She gazed at it, her fingers stroking the material as gently as if it were the baby itself.

"I can shop. Tell me or I'll be forced to bring back my idea of breakfast." Which was, most days, lunch.

"Sweets, fruit, coffee." She shrugged. "Anything."

He stood at the door a long time, watching her, telling himself to go. When he finally moved, it wasn't to leave, though. He went to the bed, cradled her face in both hands and kissed her fiercely, as if he owned her.

More truthfully, as if she owned him.

Then he left.

His first stop was the condo, where he showered, shaved and dressed. The housekeeper had been in the day before, and the place smelled clean and new. There was no cookie scent lingering in the air, no Anamaria scent in the bathroom or the bedroom, no candle scent or wooden-chest scent. No sex scent.

The fact that he even noticed made him frown as he left again through the garage.

Not much was open yet in town—the convenience stores, the truck stop on the edge of town, the twenty-four-hour doughnut shop. He settled for the bakery, a shabby little place on a side street where Sara had always bought fresh bread after Sunday-morning services. Every birthday cake that had ever graced his family's table had come from there, and his mother was insisting that when Mitch's little girl turned one in June, they had to make the trip from Mississippi for the cake.

That was a tradition worth keeping. Never marrying just because none of your relatives had done it didn't even begin to make the list.

Not that he was thinking about marriage, and certainly not with Anamaria.

He was standing at the counter, selecting enough pastries for the whole Duquesne family, when Tommy came in. He wore shorts and a T-shirt, both as soaked with sweat as his hair, and he was breathing hard.

"You're out early," Robbie commented. Tommy ran five miles most mornings, but he didn't usually hit the bakery for another hour—a detail Robbie knew secondhand since he was never out this early, either.

"Screw you," Tommy muttered, then jerked his chin toward the man behind the counter. It could have been a greeting but instead was shorthand for the usual: two jelly doughnuts and a cup of black coffee.

"Man, if giving up cigarettes makes you this much fun in the morning…"

Tommy scowled more fiercely. "I'm about as much fun as you were when you gave up booze. Where've you been?"

"Home."

"And you woke up six hours early with a craving for yeast and sugar?"

"Yeah, well, I couldn't find a good pulled pork sandwich this early."

"How's Anamaria?"

"How's Ellie?" Robbie shot back. When Tommy's gaze narrowed, he immediately regretted the question. He knew things were rough between Tommy and Ellie because he was their friend, and that made him a bastard for asking like that. "Look, I didn't mean... I wanted to ask you something."

Tommy picked up his breakfast and moved to a table. After paying for a box of doughnuts and two large coffees, Robbie followed him. He sat there a moment, listening to an old man in overalls order a dozen cake doughnuts, before finally blurting out his question. "How bizarre would it be if Glory Duquesne's baby had lived?"

Tommy chewed a bite of doughnut, then washed it down with coffee while he considered it. "About the only way that'd be possible is if she wasn't alone out there. And if she wasn't, if someone took her baby and left her there..." He shook his head grimly. "Damn. Why do you ask?"

Robbie told him about their visit to the river the night before, about Anamaria's inability to sense any hint of the baby, about Glory's missing shawl and the note for a six-thirty appointment with the unknown Lodge.

"Jeez, let me go to the lieutenant and tell him I want to take a look at a decades-old accidental death because the victim's psychic daughter can't feel the life force from her newborn sister at the scene. And, oh yeah, the victim's shawl is missing."

It sounded as ridiculous as Robbie had expected. Still, he argued the point. "To hear Anamaria tell it, the shawl is like that medal you wear. It's a family thing—and these people are *big* on family. They've got this intense matriarchal-society thing going on that makes our families look like slackers at staying in touch."

Tommy's jaw tightened at the mention of the medal, but he didn't reach for it or tuck it inside his shirt. His mother had put it around his neck when he was seven, then she'd left to go to the store and had never been seen again. And Robbie had never seen him without the medal since.

"A shawl," he repeated. "That's something you wrap around you, right? No buttons, no zippers? It could have fallen off. It could be out there in those woods under a pile of dead leaves. Or it could have dropped into the river."

"Or, if somebody was there with Glory, he could have wrapped it around the baby."

"And what did he do with the kid?"

Robbie shrugged. "Raised her as his own. Gave her to someone else. Sold her to someone else."

Tommy swiped jelly from his fingers before picking up the second doughnut. "It's a better scenario for the kid than drowning or being eaten by wild animals. But it's still pretty far-fetched."

"But it's possible."

This time it was Tommy who shrugged. "Anything's possible. 'There are more things in heaven and earth…'" After a moment, he grinned. "I was watching PBS last night."

The coincidence made the hairs on Robbie's neck bristle. Shakespeare again, first from an elderly fortune-teller, and now a cop who'd squeaked through high school English lit by the skin of his teeth—just for the sake of the football team.

"The way I see it, there are only two ways to prove it. Find the person who was there and get him to admit that he left Glory to die, that he maybe even helped her along before disappearing with her baby. Or find the baby and compare her DNA to Anamaria's." Tommy polished off his doughnut, opened Robbie's box and chose a cream cheese-glazed cinnamon roll. "He couldn't have stayed here in town with the baby. That would have been too obvious, especially with teams searching the river for days."

"Wouldn't she have needed medical care right away?"

"I don't know, man. Do I look like I know anything about babies? If she did, he couldn't have taken her to a hospital within two hundred miles of here. Too big a risk. But a private doctor…"

Some doctors would do anything for the right amount of money.

Or the right patient.

Several of the names Marguerite had given them the day before came from enough money and influence to qualify on both counts. Robbie and Anamaria needed to start making lists and ruling out whoever they could. It still might be impossible to figure out who fathered Charlotte, or if he'd had anything to do with Glory's death, but it was all they had at the moment.

"I'll talk to you later," he said, rising abruptly, picking up his box and coffees. "Tell El—" Annoyed, he shook his head. It was just habit: *Tell Ellie hello; tell Ellie to come with you next time.* He wished they'd stay together or apart, because the on-again, off-again crap was too much hassle.

With a scowl, Tommy dismissed the blunder. "Later."

After a stop at his office, Robbie returned to Easy Street more than an hour and a half after he'd left. Anamaria was dressed in denim jeans that ended just below her knees and a worn T-shirt advertising some herb festival in Savannah. She sat at the kitchen table, Glory's notebooks piled in front of her, one open. The baby bonnet was carefully laid out beside them, and her fingers idly stroked the fine fabric.

A glance through the door into the next room showed that the bed was made, its covers straightened, its pillows piled high. He'd rather rumple it again than talk about the matter at hand, but he joined her at the table.

"The coffee's cold."

She smiled faintly. "I made a pot. You take longer to shower and dress than Auntie Charise's twin girls. Believe me, that's saying a lot."

"I ran into Tommy, and I stopped by the office." He set down the bakery box, along with a file folder, then went to the counter and poured himself a cup of coffee. "Did you find anything in the appointment book?"

Her expression was blank for a moment; then her gaze darted guiltily toward the bonnet. "Uh, no, sorry. I was just thinking..."

About her mother. Glory Duquesne may have been dead most of Anamaria's life, but she wasn't gone. She lived on in her daughter's heart. She'd handled the things in that chest, filled the notebooks with the details of her work and tied that bonnet underneath Anamaria's baby chin, maybe Jass's and Lillie's, too, and had planned to do the same with Charlotte. She'd lived and loved and had had a huge impact on the people who'd lived with her and loved her back.

He topped off her coffee, sat down, took a maple bar from the bakery box and checked the front of the notebook she'd chosen. Atlanta, where Glory had lived when she had gotten pregnant with Anamaria. Had the father been one of her clients? Did Anamaria hope to find his name in one of those pages?

He chose the Copper Lake notebook and opened it to the first pages. Appointments were sparse in Glory's first few months in town; like any profession, he supposed, it took time to build a following. He'd been lucky; he'd come out of law school about the time his uncle Cyrus had retired and had been given all of the old man's clients, including Calloway Industries, the county's largest employer.

Most of Glory's early clients had been neighbors; he recognized their names from the city directory list he'd pulled the day before. Gradually, her base had spread outside the neighborhood, and soon the appointments were scattered with other notations: initials, dates and dollar signs. Most of the initials matched names on Marguerite's list.

Distaste knotted his gut. Was that how Glory had paid for this house and supported Anamaria? Having sex for money?

"We prefer to think of it as a business arrangement," Anamaria said quietly, as if she'd read his mind. But she wasn't a mind reader, or so she said. "The gentlemen get attention, sex, satisfaction, secrecy and, if they want, exclusivity, and in return they pay a reasonable sum."

He thought of his conversation with Mama Odette last night, her remark about Anamaria entertaining a gentleman, and the roll he'd eaten turned heavy in his stomach. No wonder she'd realized right away that he'd been intimate with her granddaughter; no wonder she'd taken no offense. She'd assumed that they had an arrangement, that he would pick up this month's expenses for her girl, make a deposit into her bank account or gift her with extravagant jewels, or clothing.

Mama Odette had assumed wrong.

"Yeah, if I were conducting criminal activity, I'd rather think of it as a business arrangement, too," he said snidely.

Her color drained, leaving her unusually pale. "Criminal activity?"

"Charging for sex is illegal, Anamaria. It's called prostitution."

"My mother wasn't a prostitute." The color flared back, as obvious in her voice as her cheeks. "She was mistress to a number of men—I admit that. But that's different. I bet someone in every generation of your family has had a mistress, right up to your father."

He couldn't deny that. Sex and support—that was exactly

the relationship Gerald had had with Mitch's mother, and she wasn't the only other woman. Just the only one to get pregnant.

What about *him?* Was he supposed to offer her a few hundred bucks, a few grand? Were the first couple of times free, and then she expected him to pay up? It wasn't going to happen. He'd never paid for sex, and he wasn't starting now. "What about you?"

Her head came up regally, and her gaze turned icy. He recalled the African Greek goddess image, soft and approachable—and only a memory. This was African warrior woman. If he tried to touch her now, he was liable to draw back a bloody stump. "You call me a prostitute, Robbie Calloway, and I'll carve out your heart with a dull knife. You offer me money to be your mistress, I'll put a curse on you that not even Mama Odette can remove. Do you understand?"

He tried to lighten her anger. "I thought you were just into the psychic-readings-cards stuff. Curses seem to be more heavy-voodoo stuff."

She pointed one finger at him, the buffed nail inches from the tip of his nose, and borrowed Mama Odette's accent. "You be surprised what we can do, chile."

She stared at him, and he stared back before deliberately capturing that warning finger, and her hand, in his. "I'm not one of your gentlemen."

With little effort, she managed to twist her fingers so her nails pinched into his skin. "I've never *had* any gentlemen. I take care of myself, and when I have my daughters, I'll take care of them, too. I won't be any man's mistress."

Or wife. And that was a shame—for her, for those daughters and for the men who fathered them.

An unwelcome thought, sad and disquieting, settled over him.

It might be a shame for him, as well.

Chapter 8

Anamaria ate doughnut holes while watching Robbie skim through the Copper Lake journal. She knew what he was looking for; it could have been a category on a game show: Last Names Beginning with the Letter *C*. How badly would he react if he found any of his relatives in there, particularly with a dollar sign after them?

He wouldn't call her mother a prostitute again, she thought stiffly, especially if it turned out that his relatives were among her clients.

Could they discover anything else that would make her even more unsuitable in his eyes? Good thing she'd come into this affair knowing there was no hope for the long-term, or her heart would be hurting right now. Even knowing what to expect, she felt a faint twinge.

He paused on a page about halfway through the notebook. "Here's where she started seeing Lydia. And two weeks later, here…" His voice trailed away, his finger tapping a place on the page.

Anamaria walked around the table to look over his shoulder. *C. Calloway, 9 a.m.* Uh-oh. Aiming for breeziness, she bumped her hip against his shoulder. "Making love in the morning. Imagine that."

He snorted, then moved his finger to reveal the phone number jotted below the name. "That's my uncle Cyrus. If he hadn't had a son who looked just like him, I'd have thought he'd never had sex. He was a cold old bastard who had little time or regard for anyone, especially his wife and son. If he had an affair with your mother, she was a miracle worker in disguise."

"Doesn't sound as if he's the psychic-reading type. Why else would she have met with him?"

Robbie looked up at her, a grim smile on his lips. "He was Harrison Kennedy's lawyer at the time."

That was where she'd heard the name: when she'd told Lydia that her husband had his attorney investigating her, Lydia said he'd done the same thing with Glory. "Déjà vu."

He slid his arm around her waist and pressed his face briefly to the swell of her breast. "Except that the first thing I noticed about you was how damned beautiful you are and how damned much I wanted you. I doubt Uncle Cyrus even noticed your mother was a woman."

"Oh, men noticed Glory," she disagreed. "Even dead ones."

She saw his rueful smile as he turned back to the notebook. He didn't believe, but he was showing it less. Amazing what a taste of Duquesne passion could do for a man's tolerance.

While he read, she stroked his hair, dark, silky, never unruly. His arm around her felt so right. His bringing coffee and dough-nuts. Waking up with him. Going to bed with him. Having sex with him. Talking with him. All of it felt so damn right.

And why not? It was destiny.

But losing it all, giving it up, not fighting for him...as he'd insisted earlier, that was merely tradition. Assuming this was all she could have—a few days, sex, a baby—was cowardly. Expecting nothing more was just plain wrong.

"This is interesting." He gestured to another entry. "*LK 2:15*. That's Lydia Kennedy. Then in the margin, with a different pen, she wrote *K & S Calloway*."

"Sounds like another law firm."

He shifted his chair back to make room for her, then settled her on his lap. "Actually, I'm guessing that's my mother, Sara, and my cousin, Kent. Mom and Lydia have been best friends all my life, and Kent's Lydia's nephew. She's been more of a mother to him than his own mother ever was." He shook his head in disbelief. "My mother seeing a psychic. Jeez. I didn't see that one coming."

The second message Anamaria had delivered to Lydia had involved Kent: Mr. John was concerned about him. He was an only child born to selfish parents and, in Lydia's opinion, had suffered sorely for it. But he hadn't gone hungry; he hadn't been beaten; as a boy, he hadn't stood by and watched strangers lower either parent into the ground for eternity. Things could have been worse.

Though wasn't it easier for her to know that her mother had died loving her than for him to know his mother was alive and well and just didn't care?

Seeking distraction, she nuzzled Robbie's neck. He smelled of expensive soap, shampoo and cologne, and the fine fabric of his shirt and trousers was expertly tailored, but the extravagances were just extras. She would be just as attracted to him if he washed with dish soap and wore nothing at all. Maybe even more so.

He swatted her butt as if he knew her mind was wandering. "Concentrate. We've got a meeting with Marguerite before too long, so there's not time for that."

"You be amazed what I can do in ten minutes, chile," she murmured.

His features formed a frown. "Imitating your seventy-year-old grandmother is *not* the way to turn me on."

She snorted. "Something as simple as breathing turns you on." Then, because they did have an appointment, she slid from his lap and returned to her chair. "Glory did most of her readings here at the house, out on the front porch if the day was nice. But some of her clients weren't comfortable coming to Easy Street. Lydia's lived her entire life in Copper Lake and has probably never set foot in this neighborhood." The same could likely be said of Sara Calloway.

"So Glory went to Lydia's house."

Anamaria nodded. "I imagine that day your mother just happened to drop in while Glory was there. And Lydia said, 'Sit down, Sara Sue, and let Glory tell your fortune.' Same with Kent. It becomes like a parlor game, like doing magic tricks. No one takes it seriously, not even the reader. In that moment, it's nothing but entertainment."

Robbie's dark gaze fixed on her, level and measuring. She thought over what she'd just said, realized it was the name that had given him pause, then shrugged. "I probably heard it somewhere."

He smiled thinly. "Her name is really Sara Ann. No one calls her Sara Sue except Lydia."

"Then that's probably where I heard it."

"Except she doesn't do it around anyone but family."

So she'd *known* it. No big deal. All her life she'd known things, a lot of them far more important than someone's nickname for her best friend. But it was a big deal to Robbie. He didn't question her further, but he was wondering, and that was a good thing. An open mind was…well, open to change, new experiences and different ideas. A closed mind was hopeless.

"I picked this up from the office," he said at last, handing her a manila folder.

She accepted the folder and got comfortable on the padded chair. The folder was unmarked, the pages inside a decades-old portion of Harrison Kennedy's file. She didn't wonder about the legalities of sharing a client's record with her but read Cyrus's notes from the initial meeting with Harrison. Sounded familiar, she thought drily: find out what he could about Glory, keep an eye on her and don't be discreet. Like Robbie, Cyrus had done a thorough investigation—on Glory, her background, her family and her men. He'd met with her on multiple occasions and had found nothing obvious to force her from Copper Lake or Lydia's life.

Had Cyrus been attracted to Glory, as Robbie was attracted to her? Even coldhearted bastards had blood flowing through their veins that burned hot from time to time.

Had Cyrus begun an affair with Glory, like Robbie had with her?

Just the thought sent shivers of distaste down her spine. *Déjà vu*, she'd said earlier. Too much so.

She learned nothing from the file except that Cyrus was a compulsive note taker. *Ms. Duquesne arrived six minutes past the appointed time. Ms. Duquesne rescheduled less than an hour before the appointed time. Eighteen minutes into the meeting, Ms. Duquesne refused to supply references and walked out. Glory twenty-eight minutes late due to client "emergency." Rescheduled for 7 p.m. tonight.*

That meeting was the last one documented. Anamaria looked at the date. "Check the month of May after the meetings with Lydia started. Does Cyrus Calloway appear?"

Robbie flipped ahead a few pages. "C.C. That's probably him."

"With a dollar sign after it?"

"Two of them. Jeez, the old man was one of her clients." He shuddered. "Thinking of him having sex is like picturing my grandparents doing it."

Déjà vu all over again. What had happened between Glory and Cyrus? Had their business arrangement run its course? Had she felt anything for him besides the affection she'd felt for all of her clients? Had he felt anything for her? Or had he just used her to scratch an itch, as Mama Odette put it?

Did Robbie feel anything for *her?* He was jealous, but that had little to do with feelings and more with entitlement. He kissed her and made love to her as if she mattered, but that was passion. The women in her family had turned stirring men's passion into an art form.

He liked her. If she weren't a reader, he'd like her more. If her family were more respectable, if she weren't solidly lower-class, if there weren't black and Latina blood mixed with her white heritage…

If she were a different person, he might even love her.

Jaw tightening, she forced her attention back to the subject. "How often are Cyrus's initials in there?"

"Twice the first week, then once a week for three months. Man, I never would have believed the old man was capable of it." He flipped through the rest of the pages, then looked up. "Did she ever have sex with men she didn't charge?"

What did it say about her family that the question struck her as totally reasonable? "If she was like the rest of the family, yes. Auntie Charise and Auntie Lueena had gentlemen and boyfriends. One paid, and one didn't. One was business, and the other was personal."

Like the two of them. Robbie's reasons for coming around

had to do with business; Harrison Kennedy was paying him to keep an eye on her. Her reasons for letting him continue to come around were very personal.

"There are some notations in here—first names or initials, times always in the evening and no mention of money," he went on. "Just a pretty young woman going out on dates?"

"Probably."

His gaze locked on hers, dark and intense. "Do you date?"

Jealousy, such a primal instinct. It took so little for a man to think he had the right to be jealous, so little to stir him once he'd convinced himself of the right. Any other men in Anamaria's life were two hours away, out of sight and obviously, considering the time she'd spent with him, out of mind. But he still wondered. It still stung him a bit.

And she still found a small bit of pleasure in that.

"I do date," she said, rising from the table to rinse her coffee cup and leave it in the sink. "For a woman who's cursed not to marry, I date a lot. In fact, I'd guess the curse is one of the reasons I'm popular. Everyone in the neighborhood knows about the Duquesne women. We're available and destined to stay that way. A good time, with no expectations."

He brought his own cup over, reaching past her to set it in the sink. "You sell yourself short."

Smiling, she shook one finger at him. "At least you didn't say cheap."

"I like my heart where it is, thank you." He moved closer, blocking her in so she couldn't move without effort, then nuzzled her ear. "The men in Savannah are fools."

She shivered as his tongue traced the outer rim of her ear, but still she disagreed with him. "They want a diversion, and when they're done, they move on. Duquesne women are fun, sexy and perfect for a fling. But for a serious relationship, a marriage, a family, the men look somewhere else. For someone more suitable. Someone more conventional." She paused before softly adding, "Just like you."

His muscles went stiff, and emotion radiated off him as his startled gaze met hers. He didn't deny anything she'd said, though. In fact, his stricken look confirmed what she'd understood from the beginning: she could never be more than an affair to him. She was all wrong for a Calloway. In her family, differences were embraced. In his family, they caused embarrassment.

She eased away from him and picked up several plastic-wrapped plates of cookies, then added the stack of notebooks from the table. "We should leave soon or we'll interfere with Marguerite's show again," she said quietly.

Her footsteps echoed hollowly as she went through the house, locking windows. By the time she'd secured the last one, Robbie was waiting for her by the door, looking as if he needed to say something and having no clue how to say it. Since she was sure it was an apology, she didn't care to hear it.

After pointedly waiting for him to step outside, she locked the door, then crossed the porch and stepped outside the screen door. It was a warm day, the sky blue without so much as a streak of clouds, and the humidity hovered unseen, a thick moistness that added to the heat.

She didn't offer to drive her own car but walked to the Vette with him. Cookies balanced in her lap, she stuffed the notebooks in her bag as they drove in silence to the nursing home—backstreets again, she noticed—where they walked down the long hall to Marguerite's door.

There Anamaria stopped and held out a plate of cookies. "Why don't you take these to Tommy's grandfather? Tell him a friend made them. We can pass as friends, can't we?"

"Damn it, Anamaria—" He broke off when an aide came out of the next room, giving them a curious look, then he took the cookies and strode across the hall, rapping sharply at Mr. Maricci's door.

Marguerite sat near the window again, the roses from their last visit on the sill beside her. She exclaimed over the cookies, professing to a sweet tooth that got worse with age, and asked about Robbie.

"I made this for you," she said, picking up a notepad from the bedside table with a trembling hand. It took a second try to lift the top pages, then tear them off. "That's everyone I could think of that knew Glory. Gentlemen, boyfriends, clients. People at church, people in the neighborhood."

Anamaria scanned the spidery writing, recognizing a fair number of the names from the journal. Folding the pages in half, she asked, "Did you know that Glory planned to name the baby Charlotte?"

Marguerite's wrinkled face wreathed into a smile. "That's the closest she ever came to telling me who that child's daddy was, when she said was gonna name the baby after him." Slowly the smile faded and her brow furrowed. "Ain't no Charleses on that list. No Carls, either. Isn't that odd."

"Maybe he didn't live here in town."

"Would've had to been a travelin' man, then, because your mama, she didn't go nowhere. Just down to Savannah to see her mama and sisters three or four times a year. More likely, it's a middle name or a family name. If his name was George and she named her baby Georgina, there wouldn't be much secret there, now, would there?" Her smile reappeared. "And Glory did like the secret. For her, it would have been enough that she knew the connection between the baby's name and the daddy. It wouldn't have mattered if anyone else got it."

Keeping a secret for her own satisfaction—that sounded like Glory.

"Miss Marguerite, the night that Glory passed...do you think there's any chance that Charlotte lived?"

The elderly woman's eyes widened, and she raised one hand to the lace hankie pinned to the collar of her robe. "I never saw how it could be possible, but, honey, you said all through that night that your mama was dead and your sister was gone. Not passed. Not dead. Just gone. I thought maybe you was a little confused, or maybe just too young to understand the difference. But a funny thing—you said the shawl was gone, too. And sure enough, when the police found her, t'weren't no shawl. No sign of it anywhere." She sighed. "Me and some of her friends, we tramped through those woods and we waded through the water at the river's edge from where she was found all the way down past town. We knew that shawl was important to her family, to you. But we never found nothin'."

Robbie had slipped inside Marguerite's room in time to hear the last of their conversation. Was it odd that Anamaria was willing to take so much more on faith than anyone he knew and yet needed cold, hard proof of her sister's death? The police department had looked at the possible explanations and chosen the likeliest, and everyone but Anamaria had accepted it. But *possible* and *likeliest* weren't definitive. There was no proof that Charlotte had died; there was no proof that she lived. Why shouldn't Anamaria believe what was best for her? Was never seeing her hopes fulfilled any worse than giving them up without a battle?

"What next?" Anamaria asked when they left the room a short time later.

"Let's go see Lydia." He'd been forbidden to talk to Lydia about Anamaria or her mother, but the conversation would be ended long before Harrison found out. What would he do then? Fire Robbie? That wouldn't change a thing he was doing.

Twin Oaks was a couple of miles east of town. The Federal house stood in the center of a thousand acres or so of its original holding, with massive live oaks anchoring the front at each side. Lydia's Cadillac was parked under a smaller oak to the left; so was a familiar red SUV.

Robbie considered swinging the wheel in a U-turn and heading back to town. He didn't want to disturb Lydia when she had company, he could say. But her visitor wasn't a visitor at all; she was more like family to Lydia—and she was definitely family to him—and if Anamaria ever found out, she'd be disappointed. Damn it, he didn't like the way that made him feel.

He parked beside the SUV, then gestured toward the rear of the house. "They'll be in the gardens out back."

Their steps crunched on the gravel drive as they followed it past the house and hedges. At the first path, they turned to the right, then followed the voices beyond multiple gardens and a fountain before they reached the small nook framed by azaleas that circled a teak table and four chairs. Lydia occupied one, wearing a long-sleeved shirt and a floppy hat and fiddling with a pair of gloves.

Robbie's mother, Sara, sat in the other.

"Hey, Miss Lydia, Mom." He kissed both women on the cheek, then stood back to draw Anamaria in closer so he could perform introductions.

"Miss Lydia. Mrs. Calloway," she said politely.

"You can call me Sara," his mother replied, then raised her hand before Anamaria could respond. "Not Miss Sara. Just plain Sara."

"Oh, shoot, now you make me look old-fashioned," Lydia fussed. "I like being called Miss Lydia by the young folks."

"It is old-fashioned, but enjoy it if you do. Just don't sentence the rest of us to it," Sara said. "Come have a seat, Anamaria. I've heard a lot about you."

Anamaria slipped between Robbie and the bushes to reach the chair his mother gestured to. She missed the look Sara gave him—measuring, curious. Disapproving? What had she heard about Anamaria, and who had she heard it from? Not him, which was likely one of her complaints.

"You sit, too," Lydia commanded, nudging the remaining chair toward him as she pulled a cell phone from her pocket and notified the cook that there would be two guests for lunch.

There was a time not so very long ago, when Robbie's grandparents were young, that a servant would have been hovering nearby for the sole purpose of delivering messages and refilling tea glasses, and a time before that when it would have been a slave. When Lydia's family—when his own family—had *owned* people like Anamaria's family. What did Anamaria think about that? Was she half as uncomfortable with the idea as he suddenly was?

"So, Anamaria, tell me about yourself," Sara invited. "You're Glory Duquesne's daughter, and you probably don't remember much about Copper Lake, since you were so young when you left. We met once, if I recall, right here. Lydia had an appointment with Glory, and I barged in. She read my cards and answered a few questions for me."

Shaking off the disquiet, Robbie asked, "What kind of questions?"

"The usual for a woman my age, I imagine. Would I fall in love? Would I remarry? Oh, and would you boys ever settle down and act like civilized human beings before my hair turned white?" Sara smiled at the memory. "She told me to invest in hair coloring."

He found the other questions more interesting. He'd always seen Sara as his mother. Not a woman, and certainly not a woman who missed dating, making out, having sex. But truth was, she'd been only thirty-six when Gerald had died. Too young to spend the rest of her life alone, too young to give up being a woman, to settle for just her roles as mother and, now, grandmother. But here she sat, as alone as the day Gerald had died. Robbie couldn't recall her going out on a single date, or even remember her looking at any man with interest.

He didn't *want* to see her looking at any man with that kind of interest. She was his *mother,* for God's sake. But he wanted her to be happy.

"Perhaps if she were here today, she'd tell you to quit keeping Mr. Greyson at a distance and accept one of those invitations he's been offering." Anamaria smiled serenely. "She would probably recommend the cruise, though the picnic might be a better first date."

Sara's face flushed red, and Lydia gave a whoop of amazement. "You never told me he asked you to go on a cruise! That dirty old man!"

"Who the hell is Mr. Greyson?" Robbie demanded.

"Watch your language," Sara said, swatting at him but so distracted that she missed. "He's just a man who's been coming to church the past few months. He lives in Augusta, but he's planning to move here, once he finds a suitable place, so he's spending weekends here. And he was very clear that we would have separate cabins." Her face grew redder as she spoke, until she threw up both hands. "Why am I telling you this? You're my son. I don't have to answer to you."

"You're thinking about running off on a romantic cruise with a total stranger? Oh, yes, you do. Do the others know about this guy?"

"If any of you bothered to come to church on Sunday mornings, you would have met him for yourself. But, no. I haven't mentioned it to any of them." Her gaze sharpened. "To *anyone* except Lydia."

"Don't look at me that way," Lydia said. "I've been keeping your secrets since second grade. I didn't snitch."

"So…" Sara drank deeply of her tea before managing a semblance of calm and facing Anamaria. "I understand you're trying to find out something about your mother's time here. Are you having any luck?"

"Some."

"She was a lovely woman. I only spoke to her a few times, but she certainly seemed to have no shortage of m—friends."

Men, she'd been about to say. She didn't know the half of it, Robbie thought. He met Anamaria's gaze, his brow quirked and she nodded imperceptibly. He leaned forward, resting his arms on the tabletop, and casually asked, "Did either of you know that Uncle Cyrus was a friend of Glory's?"

"Cyrus didn't have a friend in the world," Sara declared.

"He couldn't even relate to people he had a lot in common with," Lydia added. "What interests could he possibly have shared with Glory?"

Robbie cleared his throat uncomfortably. "He was a man. She was a beautiful woman."

Sara and Lydia looked at each other and burst into laughter. "Cyrus? Having sex? Oh, please!"

Lydia wiped tears from her eyes. "If that boy didn't look just like him, I'd have sworn it was a case of immaculate conception. My sister never knew whether to resent or rejoice that he had no interest in sex. On the one hand, it doesn't make a woman feel too good that her husband doesn't want her, but on the other hand—"

"When that husband was Cyrus," Sara added, and the laughter began again.

After a time, Lydia gave a heaving shudder. "Oh, my. That old goat was old enough to be Glory's daddy, and out chasing her like he had a right. No wonder Mary danced on his grave."

To the best Robbie could recall, Mary had been vacationing in Europe when Cyrus died, and she had made it home only hours before the funeral. She'd stayed long enough to accept everyone's condolences and to hear the will, then had retired to a friend's villa in Tuscany to grieve in private.

Not that anyone had really grieved. Not Cyrus's brothers and sisters, not his nieces and nephews, and certainly not his son and grandson. He'd been a difficult man to endure. Glory wasn't the only one who'd required payment to put up with him.

"Do you think Mary or Kent knew?" Sara asked.

Lydia shook her head. "Heavens, no. Mary would have told me, after she'd flayed Cyrus alive. And Kent…he would have told me, too, I think. He kept a secret or two, but they were about the girls in his own life. Anything about his father, he eventually told me. Lord, even today this would upset Kent. His daddy always giving him hell about what he did and who he saw, and the whole time he was out screwing around with a wh—"

Abruptly Lydia froze, and the color in her face matched the red in her gloves. Sara was stricken, too, her eyes wide. Anamaria's color was heightened, though Robbie doubted anyone could tell but him. Her expression was polite, almost serene, but underneath sparked anger in her mother's defense.

"Oh, Anamaria, I'm *sorry*," Lydia said, laying her hand on Anamaria's. "I just forgot who we were talking about. I was thinking about the kind of woman who would get involved with Cyrus and let my mouth get ahead of my brain. But I adored Glory, you know I did, and I'm sure she had her reasons. I'm so sorry."

"It's all right, Miss Lydia," Anamaria said, without so much as a hint of the stiffness that held her rigid a moment earlier. "I'm sure she did have her reasons."

Yeah, like keeping a roof over her head and providing food for her daughter. A regular job would have been more respectable, but Glory had never held one of those, according to Cyrus's notes in Harrison Kennedy's file. Besides, being a mistress paid better for a woman with no job skills beyond her psychic gifts and making a man happy.

Apparently, she'd made a *lot* of men happy.

"Well…well…" Lydia fluttered her hands. "Let me go see what's taking so long with lunch. Y'all stay right here."

"Why don't you go with her, Robbie?" Sara suggested. "You can help carry everything out."

He looked from Sara to Anamaria, then back again, reluctant to leave them alone. His mother wore a look he knew well—shrewd, determined, judging—and Anamaria wore another he well knew—stubborn. Whatever conversation Sara was intent on having would happen whether he stayed or went, so, like a coward, he stood up and aimed for humor. "Do you know how much of my life you've spent sending me away so the grown-ups could talk?"

"I'm not trying to get rid of you. I just think men should make themselves useful whenever possible. Don't you agree, Anamaria?" She barely waited for Anamaria's nod. "Go on. Be useful."

Robbie bent close to her. "Don't interrogate her and don't intimidate her," he murmured.

Sara's smile was charming and sunny…and pure bull. "We're just going to talk. Go. Now."

Like a good son, he went. And truthfully, he was glad to be going.

"I was a single mother long before my husband died. I raised three sons full-time and a fourth one part-time," Sara said after Robbie was out of hearing range. "I'm very good at interrogation and intimidation. I had to be. But I really do just want to talk."

Anamaria believed everything up to the last sentence. Since she'd never had a serious relationship, she didn't have much experience meeting men's mothers. There had been a few boyfriends from the neighborhood whose mothers she'd known since she was little, but they knew about the Duquesne family curse, so they never felt compelled to "talk."

Of course, Sara didn't know there was anything between Anamaria and Robbie besides Glory's last days in Copper Lake. She couldn't possibly guess they were lovers, and even if she did, she undoubtedly knew that her youngest son would never get seriously involved with someone so unsuitable for their family.

For a moment, Sara gazed into the distance, and Anamaria took the opportunity to look around as well. The garden was large, probably five or six acres stretched between the rear of the house and an impressive gazebo at the north border. How did it compare with the garden at Calloway Plantation? The photographs in the tourism brochures were spectacular, but if the photos didn't do the house justice, the garden might be more breathtaking, too.

The only way she was going to find out was to pay her ten dollars and take the tour.

Finally Sara refocused on her, her gaze like Robbie's—blue and intense. "Did Lydia tell you about Jack Greyson?"

Anamaria shook her head.

"He's a nice man. Divorced. After thirty-three years of marriage, his wife decided it was 'me' time again. She spends her time traveling and having plastic surgery." Self-consciously Sara touched her cheek. "I don't care much about wrinkles. I've earned them. Might as well display them."

"He's not going back to his ex-wife," Anamaria said quietly. "That's over."

Sara's expression was somewhere between hope and

doubt. "I've been alone a long time. Probably as long as you've been alive. I'm pretty set in my ways."

"Mr. Greyson doesn't want to change you. He just wants to share those ways with you."

"That's what he says," she murmured. She stared a long time, not looking away even when a pickup truck drove past on the graveled road. "What do you see in your future, Anamaria?"

"I can't see my future."

"What do you see in my son's future? Or is it blocked, too, because it includes you?"

Goose bumps skittered down Anamaria's arms—what she imagined people felt the first time they experienced a true psychic moment. Sara couldn't know. Robbie never would have told her. But she could suspect and come fishing for information. "I can't read everybody, and what I see is generally just a small part of their lives."

"That's not an answer," Sara chided.

"I haven't tried to read him. I usually don't except for clients."

"So that bit about Jack and the cruise…was that a little non-believer special?"

Anamaria allowed a small smile. "That was just so easy to pick up, and I knew it would surprise Robbie, if not you."

"It surprised us all," Sara said drily. "My sons don't think of me as a woman having 'needs,' and Lydia's been happily married for forty years. I don't think they realize how lonely life can get." After a moment's reflective silence, she fixed her gaze on Anamaria again. "Are you in Robbie's future?"

"Not for long," Anamaria answered, regretfully.

"Is that his choice or yours?"

"It's no one's choice. It's…destiny." Destiny that Robbie didn't believe existed. A curse that he thought she and her family had turned into a self-fulfilling prophecy.

"You don't want to live in Copper Lake?"

"It's a nice town."

"You don't want to marry into a white family?"

"I'm white, too."

Sara nodded in polite deference. "I see that. But when I look at you and think race, I think black."

Anamaria nodded, too. She lived in a predominantly black neighborhood, with predominantly black friends. It was easier to find acceptance there, especially in a world where race was an easy way to categorize people.

"There would be a fair number of Calloways—and others—who wouldn't welcome you."

Would you be one of them?

"My boys mean the world to me. Ever since they each graduated from college, I've been anxious for them to settle down and start giving me grandbabies. It took Mitch and Russ getting married, then divorcing, to show me that it was better they wait for the right woman than to try to make it right with the wrong one." She smiled broadly. "Now I have one adorable granddaughter and two more on the way."

Three more, Anamaria thought. Even if Robbie chose not to tell her about this one. Of course, she had to tell him first. That had been one of Mama Odette's lessons: you always tell the daddy…if you know who he is.

"I guess this is just a long way of saying that if you make my son happy, then the part of the family that matters will be happy. The rest of them, as far as I care, can go suck pond water."

Footsteps approached as she finished, just one set that didn't belong to Robbie. Anamaria would have sensed it if they had. A moment later, a tall, slender man appeared in the break between azaleas. "Hey, Aunt Sara. I heard voices and thought Aunt Lydia might be with you."

"She's in the house. Anamaria, this is Lydia's and my

shared nephew, Kent. This is Anamaria Duquesne, Glory Duquesne's daughter. You remember her, don't you?"

So this was Kent Calloway, subject of Mr. John's second message to Lydia. In his early forties, blond-haired and brown-eyed, he was handsome in a faded, superficial sort of way. His father had criticized and belittled him, his mother had abandoned him, and he'd let it sink into him until bitterness and resentment hovered in the air around him. Unhappiness had become a permanent part of who he was, staining everything else about him.

He stared at her a moment before answering Sara's question. "I've heard the name. I never met her, though." He nodded curtly. "Nice to meet you. I'll catch Aunt Lydia at the house."

According to Glory's notebook, she'd done a reading for K Calloway the same time she'd advised Sara to buy stock in hair coloring. Was there another Calloway with the same initial, or had Kent been too young and disinterested to notice her?

She asked the question of Robbie as they drove away from the house two hours later, and he snorted. "He's at a table with two women old enough to be his mother and an exotic, beautiful girl only a few years older than him and he doesn't notice her?"

"Could there be another K Calloway besides Kent?"

"I don't know. My grandmother spends her spare time working on what she calls the family forest. She's got every birth and death in the family from 1800 to the present. I'll call her." After another moment, Robbie asked, "What did you and Mom talk about?"

"I told her that we were going home after lunch and I intended to make wild, wicked love to you."

His look was as chiding as his mother's voice had been earlier. "Anamaria."

"Last night you called me Annie."

"Did you like it?"

"I don't know." She liked her name, but it was a mouthful, and there were times when something shorter and sweeter, like Annie, a special name to be used by a special person, would be nice. "I'll let you know next time you use it."

He reached for her hand, his warm and calloused as it closed around hers. "What did you and Mom really talk about?"

"I told her she should make wild, wicked love to Mr. Greyson."

His grimace was exaggerated; the shudder running through him wasn't. "Jeez, this is my mom we're talking about."

"We've spent a lot of time talking about my mother and her sex life, and it didn't bother you."

"Yeah, because it's *your* mom. This is mine. If she has a sex life, I don't want to know it."

"Sara's only—what? Sixtyish? Don't you intend to still be dazzling women in bed when you're sixty?"

"Women? Plural? I'm pleased that you think I'll be capable." Raising her hand, he pressed a kiss to her palm. "But right now, I'm just looking to dazzle you."

He didn't have anything to worry about there. She was already pretty dazzled, and they hadn't even reached her house yet. If she wasn't careful, he could dazzle her right into heartache and heartbreak and loneliness too enormous to bear.

But she would manage. Duquesne women always did. It was a lesson drummed into her when she was a little girl, and it was a lesson she would start teaching her own little girl in a few years.

The only question was whether she would do the teaching alone.

Chapter 9

Her tires were flat. The rusty screens that encircled the porch had been slashed and torn. The porch furniture was upended, two legs broken off the table, and the light fixture was shattered, leaving only wires hanging from a hole in the wall. The front door had been kicked with enough force to break both the lock and a hinge, and inside, clearly visible in the dim shadows, a word sprayed in paint led off to the kitchen. WHORE.

Robbie stood at the bottom of the steps, hands knotted into fists, as fury vibrated through him. Who the hell had done this? Was the bastard a coward who'd waited for them to leave that morning, or had it just been coincidence? What would he have done if he'd found them there? Worse, if he'd found Anamaria alone there?

She sat in the front seat of the Vette, with her door open and her arms wrapped around her as if she were freezing. She didn't look so strong and serene now but hurt and frightened.

Soon enough, she would become angry. Robbie wanted her angry. Then she could deal with it.

"You have any ideas who was behind this?" Tommy asked, stepping off the porch and onto the concrete slabs below.

"We have a whole notebook full of ideas." He told him about Glory's appointment books, the customers versus the clients versus the dates.

"You didn't find your dad or mine in there, did you?" Tommy asked, only half joking. In addition to his long-term affairs, Gerald had had a lot of women like Glory. Tommy's father, on the other hand, had lived like a monk for twenty years after his wife left.

"No, but we did find Uncle Cyrus."

"That old devil?" Revulsion crossed Tommy's face. "Well, hell, let's get Mama Odette on the phone, head over to the cemetery and ask the bastard what he knows."

Robbie watched Bonnie DeLong and a couple of evidence techs working on the porch and inside the house. A few days ago, the idea of asking someone to pass on a question to a dead man would have been reason for a good derisive laugh. But if he thought for a second that Mama Odette really could contact Cyrus, he would get on the phone that quick. Though he doubted it would do any good. Cyrus alive hadn't been exactly sociable. Dead, he was likely to be downright unpleasant.

"You really believe this psychic stuff?"

Tommy put him off a minute while he talked to one of the officers, then turned back. "I heard she broke the news of your mom's new boyfriend. Where do you think she got that information? Your mom sure as hell didn't tell her. The guy, Greyson, doesn't even live around here, so odds that she found out from him are pretty slim. Lydia didn't even know part of it. So where do you think Anamaria got it?"

Robbie stared at him. "Where the hell did *you* get it?"

"You and Lydia discussed it in front of the cook, who told her daughter the dispatcher, who was repeating it to—" Tommy broke off and laughed. "There are a lot of ways to get information. For me, the gossip hotline works pretty well. You can't deny that for Anamaria there's something more at play." Without taking a breath, he switched subjects. "Are you taking her home with you?"

For an instant, Robbie stiffened. Just that morning he'd noticed that the condo smelled different from this house, totally absent of Anamaria's fragrances. If he moved her in there, even for a day or two, that would change forever. Her scents would seep into his bed, his furniture, his very walls, and after she left, her essence would linger, barely noticeable but impossible to remove.

"Afraid you can't sneak her in through the garage without the neighbors noticing?" Tommy asked with a scowl. "If you're not gonna man up, she can stay at my house."

"Screw you. Can I go in and get her stuff?"

"DeLong!" Tommy shouted. "Take him inside to the bedroom. Don't touch but what you need. And look around while you're there and see if anything obvious is missing."

Robbie nodded, glanced at Anamaria, who was gazing into the distance, then followed Bonnie across the porch. Besides the insult painted on the floor, there was no other damage inside the house. The kitchen, the bathroom and the bedroom were just the way they'd left them.

He packed Anamaria's clothes and toiletries hastily, then took the wooden chest from its place high on the shelf. Cautioning her to be careful with it, he handed the chest to Bonnie, carried the suitcases into the hall and stopped short, gazing at the dining table.

"Is something wrong?" Bonnie asked.

"There was a baby bonnet on the table when we left this morning."

"A baby bonnet?"

"Yeah. It was white and had pink ribbons." Anamaria had set it beside the notebooks that morning and had seemed a little distracted while touching it when he'd returned with coffee and doughnuts. He'd put it down to missing her mother, thinking about when *she'd* worn that bonnet and that Charlotte would have been next to wear it.

DeLong frowned. "You think someone who'd write *whore* on the floor would steal a baby bonnet?"

"I think he'd take something that obviously means a lot to the woman he'd written *whore* about."

"I'll tell the detective," she said with a shrug.

"Don't knock yourself out," he muttered. He carried the bags out to his car, then took the chest from DeLong and handed it to Anamaria. "Did you put that bonnet away when we left this morning?"

She shook her head. "I took the notebooks, but I left it on the table. Why?"

"Apparently, your vandal took it," Tommy replied.

She slid out of the seat, rising to her full height, her chin lifted. Robbie was glad to see the shock receding and anger taking its place. "He tore up my porch, called me a whore and stole an old baby bonnet?"

"Maybe the message wasn't for you." Robbie leaned against the car at her side. "We've been asking questions about your mother's lovers and about the baby's father. Maybe one of them left the message in reference to her." Only a few hours ago, Lydia had barely caught herself before calling Glory a whore, and everyone agreed that she had adored Glory. An angry ex-lover, maybe a spurned ex-lover, would likely call her that and more.

While no one in town besides Tommy, who'd probably guessed, knew that Anamaria was sleeping with Robbie.

And an ex-lover who thought that Charlotte might have been his daughter might have, for reasons good or bad, taken the bonnet.

"You guys go on, get out of here," Tommy said. "Just let me know where to reach you."

"We'll be at the condo," Robbie said. *Man up, my ass.*

"You wanna leave me your keys, Anamaria? I'll get the tires taken care of and call Russ about the rest of it."

That was something Robbie should have thought about and would have eventually, he wanted to protest as she pulled her key ring from her purse. He just had more important things—like *her*—on his mind.

After thanking Tommy, she didn't speak again until they were several blocks away. "I can stay at a motel."

"Nah. You never know who's been sleeping in those beds."

She cut him a sidelong look. "And who's been sleeping in your bed?"

"Just me. I don't usually take women home with me."

"Why not?"

"Why should I? Their places are just as convenient."

"With the added bonuses that you can leave whenever you want and your space remains your space. They don't get the chance to bring stuff over and conveniently leave it behind." She glanced at him again. "I've got *stuff,* but when I leave, I promise, I won't leave any of it behind."

The promise wasn't as reassuring as it should have been. Once they walked in the door, his space was going to be their space. Even when there wasn't a single piece of clothing, a shoe or so much as a fingerprint to indicate she'd ever been there, he would know. And he would miss her.

He typed in the code for the electronic gate, then turned

into the drive that ran along the rear of his building. His garage was on the end, neater than any other place in his life because that was where he worked on the Vette.

As the door lumbered down behind them, Anamaria looked at the tools that hung on Peg-Boards and filled chests along the walls. "You've got enough tools here for a well-stocked garage. Do you actually know how to use them?"

He gave her a wounded look before heaving her bags from the trunk. "I rebuilt this car from the frame up. When I bought her, she was a rusted heap sitting beside an old barn in southern Georgia. I did everything myself except the paint job. Where do you think I got these calluses and scars?"

"I apologize. And I'm impressed."

"My brothers and I practically grew up at Charlie's Custom Rods, out on Carolina Avenue. We've been tearing down and restoring old cars since we were kids." He grinned. "If you want to replace that bland car of yours with something deserving of a beautiful woman, I can find you the body and show you how to do it."

Cradling the wooden chest in her arms, she followed him to the door leading into the utility room, where he typed in the code on the alarm keypad. "I like that bland car of mine. Besides, that sounds like a time-consuming project. One of us would have a long commute."

"Or one of us could move to Copper Lake." He stiffened the instant he heard his own words. It wasn't the first time he'd, as Lydia put it, let his mouth get ahead of his brain. If he could take back the suggestion, he would…. At least, he thought he would. He wasn't sure.

In an effort to lessen the impact of the words, he shrugged carelessly. "The tools are here. When it comes to restoring old beauties, tools rule."

With nothing more than a barely-there murmur, she followed him through the laundry room and kitchen, past the dining and living rooms and upstairs. There were two bedrooms up there, the second not even half the size of the first. Russ had built the condos and had adapted this floor plan for Robbie. Sleepover guests would be few and far between, and Robbie had preferred the extra space for the master bedroom.

Without considering whether Anamaria might like the pretense of her own room, he carried her bags into his room. It was at the front of the house and faced the river, a wide lazy ramble at this point. The windows let in tons of light and a lot of afternoon heat, but he was rarely there then, so he kept the drapes open for the view.

Anamaria set the chest on a side table, walked to one of the oversize windows and stood, eyes closed, breathing steadily. The sunlight gleamed on her skin, giving it a burnished hue, and it softened the tension lines on her face. The goddess was back.

He set the bags down at the end of the bed, then silently moved up behind her. She didn't startle but tilted her head to one side so he could leave a line of kisses along her throat. "I believe you said something earlier about wild, wicked lovemaking."

A satisfied smile curved her mouth. "Yes. Your mother and Mr. Grey—"

Gently he nipped her lower lip, silencing her. "No mothers in this room, please. Just you and me."

"All right." Her movements slow and lazy, she twined her arms around his neck, then kissed him, her mouth hot and greedy, tasting of hunger and need and desire. She finished the kiss with her own gentle nip, then lifted her head, her gaze slumberous, her coastal accent more pronounced. "Tell me what you want, Robbie Calloway."

He looked into her eyes, the color of rich chocolate, set off so well by her mocha skin, and answered simply, "You."

One brow arched delicately. "For how long?"

"As long as we have." A day, a week, a month, a lifetime. However long, he wanted it.

She chuckled. "You sound like Mama Odette. 'We want what we want, we take what we're given, we have as long as we have.'" The humor faded, and her voice turned husky as she took his hand and pulled him to the bed. "Come to bed with me, Robbie. Take what I'm giving. For as long as we have."

It wouldn't be enough, he thought as she drew him down to the mattress with her, as she kissed him again, as their hands worked away their clothes. No matter how long they had, no matter how much she gave, no matter how much he gave back, it would never be enough.

Not until she gave her heart. Not until he found his courage.

Anamaria awakened alone in bed, the sun a purple glow on the western horizon. She wasn't the sort to awaken disoriented. Though the bedroom was dark, she knew immediately where she was. She could sense Robbie all around her.

Light filtered in from the hallway, showing her bags at the foot of the bed. Rising, she opened the larger of the two and dressed in a pair of soft cotton shorts and a ribbed tank, both in athletic gray. After a stop in a luxurious marble bathroom, she padded downstairs and through to the kitchen.

Robbie, dressed in faded khaki shorts and a Copper Lake High School baseball shirt, was removing foam dishes from a large paper bag, releasing incredible aromas into the air. "Lucky for us, Ellie delivers, because I don't cook and I don't keep enough food in the house for someone else to cook, unless canned spaghetti counts."

"Spaghetti ceases to be food once it's canned."

"Don't knock it till you've tried it, sweetheart."

"I don't have to eat dirt to know it doesn't taste the same

as Auntie Lueena's chocolate silk pie." Circling the island, she found glasses in the cabinet, filled them with ice and took two bottles of pop from the refrigerator. By the time she'd poured, he'd transferred the food to heavy pottery plates: grilled chicken breasts with roasted onions and peppers, mashed sweet potatoes and spiced green beans.

They ate at the antique oak dining table, a good-size square that seated four in ladderback chairs. She'd noticed other antiques in the house—the barrister's bookcases in the living room, the demilune table in the hallway, the desk in the sitting area of his bedroom and a very old primitive table in the upstairs hall. She didn't get vibes from furniture about the lives it had witnessed, but if she had that talent, that table would surely give her the willies.

After giving her time to make a dent in her food, Robbie spoke quietly. "Tommy called and said the guy from Charlie's Tires— he also owns Charlie's Customs Rods—will get your new tires on tomorrow. There's a two-inch gash in each one, probably from the same knife used to slash the screens. Russ fixed the door and replaced the lock, but he can't get a crew over to resand the floor and fix the light and the screens until Monday."

She took another bite of green beans, just to prove that the news hadn't ruined her appetite, then smiled politely. "Your brother's a nice guy. He must think a lot of Tommy, to answer his calls so quickly."

"He does, and he thinks very little of people who harass other people just because they can." Robbie hesitated, then asked, "Do you have any…feelings about this? Who did it? Why? What he wanted?"

She'd been thinking about what they would do when they first got home—the same thing they'd done here—and had been in a daze of arousal and desire. Robbie's curse when he'd seen the two flat tires had snatched her out of it. She'd sensed nothing major as they walked around the car, just a faint shimmer of anger.

The rage had come from the open door, radiating from the profanity scrawled down the hallway. The instant she'd seen it, her vision had gone dark and she'd swayed unsteadily. Robbie had hustled her right back off the porch and to the car to wait for the police.

"There wasn't any hatred," she said, locking gazes with him. "Just rage. Betrayal. Abandonment. I don't know who these feelings were directed at. You were probably right that it's not me. I don't tend to stir up those kinds of passions in men. It could have been meant for Glory, or someone whose life changed because of her."

"Maybe one of her ex-lovers who thought the dirty little secret of their affair had died with her, then you show up, asking questions, and he's realized that nothing's ever quite so secret after all."

She nodded. "Or Charlotte's father, whose dirty little secret might have worn diapers. And bonnets." She turned sideways in the chair and brought her knees close to her chest to watch him while he finished eating. "You know, I automatically assumed that Charlotte's father didn't want her any more than my father wanted me."

"Reasonable assumption. I've worked a lot of child-support cases, getting DNA and money from men who denied paternity even after the proof came in."

"But Glory's luck was different. Two of the three daddies wanted their daughters right from the start. Jass's father wanted to marry Mama—he wanted to have a real family. Maybe Charlotte's father wanted that, too. Maybe he envisioned this happily-ever-after family. Maybe he loved her and thought she loved him. But she refused him."

Robbie carried their plates to the sink, then returned with

a plate of dipped chocolates. She picked one and bit into it, her teeth sinking into creamy cheesecake. She groaned softly.

"That would explain the betrayal and abandonment. And taking the bonnet. I mean, your average vandal stealing a bonnet is just plain weird." He rolled his eyes. "The average vandal I've represented wouldn't even know what it was."

"He could have given Mama the bonnet in the first place. I thought it was one she'd used for the rest of us, but it was in pristine condition, and babies don't leave much pristine. According to Mama Odette, I had the habit of chewing the ribbons off everything I owned. And it was a very good quality bonnet. Our family doesn't splurge on baby clothes."

"Okay," Robbie said after downing a chocolate-covered cherry cake in two bites. "Where's the notebook? We missed something when we went through it before."

"It's in my bag." She'd laid it at the end of the island before taking the chest upstairs. "What did we miss?"

"Timing." He jumped up from the chair, brought her bag to her, then disappeared through a door under the stairs before returning with a legal pad and ink pen. "Glory was due February 21. That means she would have gotten pregnant—" he counted backward mentally "—in June. In the pages I looked at this morning, she was keeping a pretty good record of her meetings with everyone, boyfriends and gentlemen. So let's see who's listed for June."

Anamaria flipped through the notebook. Glory had started each month on a fresh page, writing the name across the top in colored ink and underlining it twice for emphasis. It seemed an expectant statement; what month with its name written in purple capital letters and bold lines underneath it could fail to be a great month? But June's ink had faded, and there seemed nothing memorable about the entries there.

It had been a busy month, and often still was. The parents

and grandparents of kids graduating from high school and college wanted to know what the future held for them; the brides and grooms marrying over the summer wanted confirmation they were making the right choice; and people whose jobs brought relocation offers sought encouragement that the new place could be home as much as the old one was.

And with all that, Glory still found the time for three gentlemen: *AL, FW* and *CC.* Cyrus Calloway.

The same three sets of initials appeared in the month of May, along with *OG,* no dollar sign attached.

For July, it was *AL, FW, CC* and *KK.* The first three paid; the last didn't.

"I don't know anyone with those initials," Robbie said. "Unless KiKi Isaacs counts. She would have been about two at the time."

"He appears on here almost every week from the beginning of July through the beginning of February."

"Is that unusual? To keep a guy around that long?"

Anamaria smiled. "Grandma Chessie—Odette's mother—stayed with the same man for thirty years. Everybody at the nursing home thought they were married, even though she refused to share a room with him. She shared his bed, though, right up until the night he died in it. He was ninety-seven, and she was ninety-two. And Mama Odette had an on-and-off thing for years. But yeah, in our family that's unusual. If we believed in getting married, we'd keep a host of divorce attorneys busy undoing what never should have been done in the first place."

"You'd probably seduce the lawyers with your unusual beauty into doing the work pro bono," he teased, then grew serious again. "I wonder if *AL* could be Lodge." He returned to the room under the stairs—a study, she presumed—and came back with a briefcase. On top was a laptop; he set it aside and booted it up. He also took another legal pad out and tossed it on the table. "Your neighbors from twenty-three years ago. No Lodges there."

Anamaria picked up the pad. Unlike her mother's handwriting, Robbie's was clean, easy-to-read masculine swoops. Her cousin, Deonne, toyed with handwriting analysis, more for her own entertainment than any serious study, but she knew the basics. What would she make of Robbie's writing? That he was strong, confident? That the obvious fact that he wrote quickly meant he had little time to spare or was ready to move on to his next adventure?

Or one of us could move to Copper Lake. His offhanded suggestion as they'd come into the house had almost cut her off at the knees. He had actually suggested she move here. *Move.* To his hometown. At least for a while.

And, for an instant, she'd actually considered it. She didn't know squat about cars, but she knew the learning would be an experience in more ways than one. She didn't even know if he'd really been talking about cars. She just knew he'd given thought—however briefly, however casually—to the future and a place for her in it.

Maybe not much of a place. Maybe still in secret. Maybe involving a regular payment like Glory's gentlemen had given her. Maybe not a place she could even consider occupying. *I told Glory she should have more pride than to lay with a man who was ashamed to acknowledge her in public,* Marguerite had told them, *but...she said it wasn't what they felt that mattered. She wanted what she wanted.*

Anamaria wanted a place in public. She wanted everyone around to know their relationship. Accepting or not, approving or not, as long as there were no ugly little secrets.

"Hey."

Under the table, Robbie's foot nudged hers, and she startled to find him watching her. Clearly he'd said something, but she didn't have a clue what.

"OG," he repeated. "Obadiah Gadney."

She followed his pointing finger to the notes he'd taken from the city directory. *Obadiah Gadney, 108 Easy St, swmll wrkr.* "Mr. Gadney? Who, along with Beulah, constitutes the neighborhood watch?" She'd gone to his house the day she'd introduced herself to the neighbors, but he hadn't been home, and she'd never gotten the chance to go back. Now she wished she'd made the effort. Besides Lillie's and Jass's fathers, she'd never met one of her mother's lovers before. "According to Beulah, he's about a hundred and twenty years old."

"Your great-grandma Chessie proved that age isn't a factor when it comes to loving Duquesne women. Besides, Mr. Gadney's probably only about seventy. That would have put him in his forties back then, about the same age as Cyrus and in a lot better shape."

"Okay, so *OG* is Mr. Gadney. And *CC*…" She wrote out the two names on the clean legal pad. "What about *FW?*" She leaned around the table to get a better look at his computer. "What are you doing?"

"Searching county databases. If it's public record in Jackman County, it's online. My uncle Garry is county commissioner, and his daughter doesn't like to come out of her room. He's worked a deal where she gets paid for getting all county records online."

"Is she phobic?"

"Just weird."

"That's sad."

He considered it a moment, then shook his head. "Nah. Just weird. Okay, we've got eleven possibilities for *FW*. My choice would be…Frank Whitford. He owned the Mercedes dealership back then, and he loved pretty things. He was married, but his wife did her best not to be in the same room with him. He was crude and vulgar, and he stepped out on her more often than her pride could bear."

Anamaria stared at him. "Do you know this kind of information about everyone in town, or just the people with money?"

"Just the people with money who haven't learned the art of negotiating. I represented Mrs. Whitford in their divorce five or six years ago. And if Whitford's our guy, then *AL* would be Andy Lutz. They were cousins and partners—Andy ran the Cadillac dealership. Frank's parents took Andy in when his folks died and raised them like twins. They did everything together, including date the same girls."

"Are they still in town?"

Robbie shook his head. "After Frank pissed off the judge and lost just about everything he'd ever owned in the divorce, he went down to Florida to start over. A few months later, Andy headed south, too. He found it too damn hard working with Frank's ex, especially when she held the majority interest in the company."

Anamaria slid from the chair and wandered into the living room, turning on the overhead light so she could study the photos on the fireplace mantel. There were the four teenage boys with Sara smiling serenely. Robbie and an elderly woman, bearing an armful of roses, outside Calloway Plantation. A casual shot of him and his brothers, their wives and Sara at a grand, but smaller home. A portrait of the second brother, Mitch, who hadn't been raised a Calloway and had no expectations to live up to, with his wife and an adorable baby girl. A wedding photo of Rick and his beautiful bride, and another of Russ at his second wedding.

Four handsome men who bore a strong resemblance to each other. The little girl, with her dark brown hair and big blue eyes, was obviously her father's daughter. Would

Anamaria's child bear that same resemblance? Would strangers look at her and say, "Oh, there's another Calloway"?

Or, more like Mitch: "There's another Calloway bastard."

What she really wanted to hear was in a universe apart: "Oh, there's pretty little Gloriane Calloway and her parents. Aren't they a beautiful family?"

"Anamaria." A pause. "Annie?"

Slowly she smiled and turned to face Robbie. "I've decided I do like it."

"But only when I use it."

"Of course." She returned to the table and dug from the bag the papers Marguerite had given her that morning. Everyone she could think of who knew Glory, the old woman had said. Mr. Gadney's name was on it, of course. Cyrus Calloway's. And linked together on the third page, Frank Whitford and Andy Lutz. "They're all on Marguerite's list. So Charlotte's father would have been your uncle Cyrus, nice Mr. Gadney, a car dealer that got run out of town or his cousin."

The selection made her shudder. "Poor Charlotte."

"Let's check that," Robbie suggested, turning back to the computer. "If Glory's naming the kid Charlotte after Charlotte's father, she had to get the idea somewhere." He ran the other three names first, probably hoping to score on one of them. Had he yet realized, Anamaria wondered, that if Cyrus was Charlotte's father, her half sister would be his cousin?

After coming up blank on the others, he typed his uncle's name into the county birth records. There it was: Cyrus Henry Calloway, born to Henry Daniel Calloway and Theresa Carlotta Morgan.

Charlotte was named for her paternal grandmother. Anamaria knew it, felt it. They didn't have to look anymore.

Robbie caught her hand and pulled her onto his lap, wrapping his arms tightly around her, and she rested her head on his shoulder. Neither of them spoke. What was there to say? *Welcome to the family?* They sat, and he rocked her just a little, and she listened to his breathing. She felt more at home at that moment than any other time or place in her life. Comforting as Mama Odette's arms were, as soothing as her hands were, here with Robbie was Anamaria's spiritual home.

For as long as they had.

Chapter 10

On Saturday morning it was Robbie's turn to awaken alone in bed. He lay on his stomach, face buried away from the sunlight, but he still smelled Anamaria's fragrance. He still felt her absence. Worse, he still felt her presence—the hour they'd made love, the hours she'd slept beside him. If she returned to Savannah, her imprint was going to haunt him right out of his home.

Unless he went to Savannah with her.

Or persuaded her to stay. How difficult would that be? And would the difficulty come from her or him?

He allowed the aroma of coffee drifting up the stairs to distract him. It was the only thing to offer for breakfast unless the chocolate-dipped cakes left over from dinner counted. As his stomach growled, he decided they definitely did.

He rolled out of bed, stepped into a clean pair of boxers and headed downstairs. As he approached, Anamaria filled another cup from the pot, then slid it across the island to him. She wore a white button-down shirt of his and socks and was bent over the island, studying different lists of names. The dessert plate stood to one side, holding one lonely-looking half bite of chocolate-coated marble cake.

"Sorry," she murmured, pushing it toward him. "Go ahead."

He ate the treat in one bite. "Find any great revelations that have eluded us so far?"

"Just a question. When my mother wrote *K & S Calloway,* we assumed it was Kent and Sara. But Kent said yesterday he'd never met Glory. And you don't know another K Calloway."

Managing not to lick his fingers hungrily, Robbie shrugged. "That doesn't mean there isn't one. We multiply like rabbits."

Her expression softened, and she glanced down for an instant. He wondered if she was thinking that the same could be said for her family. With Glory, having sex multiple times with multiple partners every month, it was a wonder she hadn't gotten pregnant every ten or eleven months.

Pregnancy wasn't something he and Anamaria had to worry about. They'd used a condom every time, finishing off her supply and starting in on his own. Still, he couldn't deny that some part of him thought the possibility might be more fun than worry. Seeing Mitch with his daughter and how Russ looked forward to his first one, and watching Jamie get rounder every day—he'd learned pretty quickly not to call her fat. Round, she might be, but she could still throw an empty water bottle with incredible accuracy.

And he couldn't deny that the only woman remotely suitable for having kids with was Anamaria. The only one who made him think about the future and family and love.

Even though his first thoughts had been *no way, too unsuitable.*

But what made a person suitable? Breeding, money, shared interests? Every nasty divorce he'd been involved in had been between people so well-suited that their marriages should have lasted through eternity. Some of the unhappiest marriages he knew were, again, between people who appeared to be made for each other.

So what if Anamaria lived elsewhere? If her career choice might be considered disreputable? If she was illegitimate, if her mother had made a profession of loving men, if her ethnic background wasn't as white-bread as his?

The people who mattered wouldn't care, and the people who cared wouldn't matter.

He didn't care. He didn't care about the things he'd thought were wrong. All he cared about were the things that were right. She was beautiful. Intelligent. Sexy. She loved her family and was kind to others. She looked at him in a way that no one else ever had. She made him feel in a way that no one else ever had.

She made him want—not just her body, not just a few days with her. She made him want a future. A chance. A life.

She snapped her fingers under his nose, and he jerked his attention back to her. "Kent said he'd never met Glory," she repeated, "but Marguerite included him on her list. I didn't pay attention last night, because she'd scratched out several names, but look. She drew a line through his name once, then retraced it, as if the line had been a mistake."

She slid the paper to him. It did look as if Marguerite had intended the name to stay on the list. He went to the phone on the wall and dialed his mother's number. "Hey, Mom, it's me. Quick question—the day you asked Glory Duquesne about your adorably well-behaved sons, was Kent there?" He was silent a moment, then said, "Thanks. That's all I wanted to know.... I don't know about dinner tonight.... Yeah, I'll ask her. Love you."

After hanging up, he returned to the island. "Yes, he was there, and she can't believe he didn't remember, what with Glory being such a pretty girl. By the way, Russ and Jamie are having dinner for the family tonight, and we're invited."

Her eyes widened a shade, pleasure flitting in, then away. "You're invited."

"*We* are invited." *Bring a date,* Russ had told him. At the time, he couldn't imagine taking Anamaria. Now he wanted to. He wanted to see if they could work with what was right between them, if he could handle what was wrong.

She nodded briskly before returning to the conversation. "What do you know about Kent?"

"I'll tell you everything in exchange for breakfast."

Abruptly a grin danced across her face. "I get to drive the high-performance toy?" At his pained look, she shrugged guilelessly. "You aren't dressed. You can't expect to go to the grocery store like that."

"You aren't dressed, either, darlin'. You go shopping like that, and Tommy's gonna have to arrest you for inciting a riot."

"He won't mind. We knew it would come to that someday."

Robbie took her hand and pulled her toward the stairs. "Let's both get dressed—then we can go out to eat. Ellie's does a pretty good breakfast, I've been told. Not that I'm usually up in time to find out."

Her steps slowed until she stood still halfway up the stairs. When he turned to face her, her cocoa eyes were shadowed. "You've avoided even driving through downtown when I'm with you, and now you want to walk into a busy restaurant with me? Why?"

Because I'm hungry? Instinctively, though, he swallowed down the words. In his experience, women didn't do well with flippant when they were serious. "Because it's right." Not an adequate answer, but the best he could give.

"For you? Or me?"

"For us."

She looked as if she wanted to argue that there was no *us*, that if there were, he wouldn't get to make unilateral decisions about them. In fact, she pointed one finger at him, a habit she'd probably learned from Mama Odette, then she lowered it again. "Mama was right," she said defiantly. "When she told Marguerite that what mattered wasn't what those men felt, but what *she* felt. She wanted what she wanted, and so do I."

"And what do you want?" he asked somberly.

She stared a moment, emotion flickering through her eyes, then she pushed past him. "Breakfast. At Ellie's. With you."

When he reached his room, she was digging through her still-unpacked suitcase, discarding clothes on the bed until she came to the dress she wanted. It was black, sleeveless and skimpy enough that he could fold it into a neat square and slide it into his pocket, like a handkerchief. Immodestly she slipped out of his shirt, wearing only tiny pink panties underneath, then tugged the dress over her head.

For all its lack of substance, there was nothing immodest about the dress. The neckline reached up to the hollow at the base of her throat. The hem stretched down to an inch or two above her knees. The fabric clung everywhere in between, but she had a body made for clinging to. She looked perfectly demure. In fact, she looked so damned demure that suddenly all he could think about was stripping the dress off again and hauling her back into bed.

"I'll be ready in five minutes," she said as she headed toward the bathroom. "Put your tongue back in your mouth and get dressed, or Tommy will have to arrest you."

"We always figured it would come to that someday," he mumbled as he took a pair of jeans from the closet.

She took longer than five minutes. He used the time to lock

up the wooden chest in the closet in his study, where he kept his hunting rifles, a few heirlooms of monetary value and a few of sentimental value. He left Glory's Copper Lake notebook with Anamaria's purse—better safe with them—and locked the others away, as well.

When she came down, it was well worth the wait. She wore black sandals to go with the black dress, and huge silver earrings dangled from her lobes. A wide matching bracelet glinted around her left wrist, and the sexiest fragrance he'd ever smelled floated around her.

Though he would have been just as dazzled without the jewelry, the makeup, the perfume.

The drive downtown took less than five minutes. He didn't look for a parking space on the square—there was no such thing on Saturday mornings—but pulled into his office lot. Anamaria glanced at the building as she got out. "This is where you work?"

"When I can't avoid it."

"Things must be backing up."

"I have a very efficient staff."

They crossed River Road and walked the few hundred yards to Ellie's. Inside they bypassed the nearly full main dining room and went to the smaller one in back. About half the tables there were filled, including one with his brother and sister-in-law.

"Aw, hell," he muttered, stopping short to make room for a waitress clearing an empty table.

Anamaria didn't need an explanation. Strangers could pick those Calloway boys out of a crowd, and she was damn sure not a stranger. She stiffened, though. "Bet you weren't counting on running into family on your first public outing with me, were you? Because that first time we came here doesn't count. You followed me, and you weren't sleeping with me."

"No, but I was thinking about it." He gave her a wry grin. "Honey, this is Copper Lake. I run into family every damn time I step outside. And I don't mind seeing Rick. It's Amanda I try to avoid."

Anamaria looked from his sister-in-law to him. "A scorned woman doesn't forgive easily."

Scorned. A mild word for what Amanda had felt. They'd been fifteen years old, and he'd treated her like scum. Worse, he hadn't even had the sense to regret it until years later. It was with her that his drinking had last gotten him into trouble—and he'd worn the bruises from Rick's fist for the next two weeks. That was when he'd stopped drinking and decided he'd better grow up. He'd had good luck with the one, but had been a slower learner with the other.

"They've noticed you," Anamaria prodded.

Pasting on a grin, he circled around the waitress and led the way to the back table. "Hey, bubba. Amanda. You guys are in awfully early." He was careful to stay out of Amanda's reach. She was smaller than he and hadn't grown up settling disagreements with a fight, but she'd worked twelve years as an exotic dancer, so she could probably kick the hell out of him.

"Robbie," they said in unison; then Rick went on. "We drove in from Atlanta last night."

Anamaria had stopped slightly behind him. Robbie placed his hand in the small of her back and drew her forward. "This is Anamaria Duquesne. My brother Rick, and his wife, Amanda."

In tandem, their gazes flickered from him to Anamaria. Amanda said a polite hello, while Rick nodded. "Why don't you join us?" Amanda asked.

There wasn't a man in town Amanda would less like to spend time with, but she tolerated him for Rick's sake. Just as the Duquesne family would tolerate him for Anamaria's sake, Robbie thought hopefully.

With a taut smile, he held her chair for her, then slid into the other empty seat. After small talk and placing their orders, he laid his hand on the back of her chair. "Did I mention, Anamaria, that along with all the scoundrels and wastrels, I've got two cops in the family? Mitch is a special agent with the Mississippi Bureau of Investigation, and Rick's with the Georgia Bureau of Investigation."

"Really." Her gaze settled on Rick. "So you solve crimes."

"I do my best. You have one in need of solving?"

"Actually, I'm in need of information."

Robbie tore a piece from the toast on Rick's plate and munched on it. "I told her I'd tell her everything there is to know about Kent in exchange for breakfast."

"Our cousin Kent?" Rick asked, then scowled. "Jeez, why would anyone want to know about him? He's a whiny-ass punk who was born without a backbone and never bothered to develop one."

Robbie gave her a wink. "Rick, Mitch and Russ come from the hardworking, committed, making-a-difference side of the family. Kent and I are in the lazy, wouldn't-amount-to-anything-if-not-for-the-Calloway-name branch."

Rick's scowl deepened. "Knock it off, bubba. Okay, so you're lazy. And you've never been particularly good at responsibility. At least you've never blamed your problems on anyone else. Everything that ever went wrong in Kent's life is his parents' fault. His father was too hard on him…. His mother neglected him…. No one was ever there for him except his aunt Lydia.

"He got kicked out of college because he drank too much—he drank too much because of his problems with his parents. His first marriage ended in divorce because his parents set a bad example for him. He couldn't relate to his kid because they'd never shown him how to be a father. Every disappointment he's had—always Cyrus's or Mary's fault."

Robbie gazed at Anamaria. "That's pretty much all there is to say about Kent. But it doesn't explain why he lied about knowing Glory."

"You want to fill us in?" Rick asked.

Robbie left the decision to Anamaria. She gazed around the table. There was nothing like being asked to tell the brother of the man you'd just fallen in love with—a cop, no less—that your mother had made a living taking money from men for sex. She still couldn't call it by its rightful name. She couldn't think of Glory, of Mama Odette, Auntie Lueena and Auntie Charise as prostitutes. They were businesswomen. Duquesne women. That, apparently, absolved them of guilt.

But Robbie's mother knew, and it hadn't made her look at Anamaria as if she had horns and a tail. *If you make my son happy,* she'd said. Surely the cop married to the ex-stripper wouldn't be less tolerant than their mother.

So she told Rick and Amanda everything—how Glory had lived, how she had died, the men with whom she'd done business, the name of Charlotte's father and Kent's lie about meeting her.

"Jeez, and we thought old Cyrus had only the one time in him," Rick said.

"Do you guys exaggerate a lot, or was he really that bad?" Anamaria asked.

"Both," Amanda answered. "Cyrus had those gorgeous Calloway eyes, a rock for a heart and a demeanor that made Scrooge as cuddly as the Easter bunny. But maybe your mother saw something different."

She'd seen dollar signs, Anamaria thought glumly. Two of them, every week for three months.

"So your mother was pretty sure that Cyrus was the baby's father, but she quit seeing him soon after," Rick said. "Was that her choice or his?"

"It goes both ways. A guy has his fling and is ready to go back to his wife, or he gets bored and wants new excitement. A woman gets tired of a man—maybe he's not as good as he thinks he is, or his money doesn't make up for his behavior. Sometimes one of them will fall for the other. He wants to leave his wife and rescue her from the sordidness of her life, or she starts to believe his promises of leaving his wife. He'll get possessive and threaten her other clients, or she'll get jealous and start calling his wife." Abruptly Anamaria realized the intensity with which Rick and Amanda were studying her, and her skin flushed. "I come from a large family with a lot of, um, business arrangements. I'm speaking from their experience, not my own."

"So Cyrus was out of the picture," Amanda picked up. "Did she continue to see other men during her pregnancy?"

"Until about five months, probably about when she started showing. That was when her, uh, arrangements ended. But she did continue dating, someone she'd started seeing right after she got pregnant. They were together every week until the beginning of February. He's identified in her journal only by the initials *KK*."

"How about the obvious?" Rick asked. He glanced around the table but saw no spark of understanding, so he filled them in. "The guy we were just talking about. Kenton Keith Calloway. If he's kept an affair with Glory secret for more than twenty years, that would be reason enough to lie to you. If he was sleeping with her at the same time his old man was..."

Anamaria felt the simultaneous wave of disgust that went around the table. "He might have been Charlotte's father. Theresa Carlotta was his grandmother—the connection is as valid for him as it is for Cyrus."

"He's certainly capable of slashing your tires and kicking in your door," Robbie agreed. "And if he was Charlotte's father—or thought he was—he'd have reason to steal her baby bonnet."

Anamaria thought of the man she'd met the afternoon before, so full of bitterness and resentment that it had radiated from him. He was a wasted soul, Auntie Lueena would have said, all the good inside him eaten away by years of wanting what he couldn't have—his father's respect, his mother's attention, the easy life he'd thought he deserved.

And Glory's love? Her daughter? Was he one of those who'd fallen in love, who'd wanted to rescue Glory and their baby and run away to a new life? And when she'd refused—Anamaria had no doubt she would have refused—had he turned on her? Bitterness and resentment could easily spawn rage; hate could make a man stand by while the woman he'd loved died. Hate could make him take their child, hide her someplace, give her to someone else and let everyone else who loved her and had a right to her believe she'd died tragically and alone.

Poor Charlotte. No matter which man had fathered her, cold cruelty and sickness ran through her veins. But Duquesne blood could overcome bad blood.

"Maybe Glory's meeting that night was with him," she murmured to Robbie, then explained to the others. "She had two appointments the night she died. One was with Lydia Kennedy. The other…" She pulled the journal from her bag and flipped through it to the loose sheet of paper, holding it out for them to see. *Tuesday, 6:30, Lodge.* "We thought maybe Lodge was a name, but we haven't come up with anyone."

Amanda took the paper and turned it over. "For what it's worth, this is Calloway Industries stationery from twenty-some years ago. My father worked for the company, and he was left a quadriplegic from an on-the-job accident. He had a letter from their grandfather thanking him for his service, framed and sitting beside the bed for the nine years it took him to die."

Rather than Kent's all-encompassing resentment, it was regret that emanated from Amanda. She may have thought her father deserved more than a letter of thanks from the elder Calloway, but it was a minor thing amid the love she'd felt for him.

"Both Cyrus and Kent would have had access to it," Rick said.

"It was Cyrus," Anamaria said at the same time Amanda spoke his name. She gestured to the other woman to go on.

"If I were a single mother about to give birth to a wealthy man's child—or grandchild—I'd be asking for money. Cyrus would have more to spare than Kent."

"And *lodge* isn't a name." Robbie tapped the paper. "Jeez, it's a place—that old fishing camp of Cyrus's upriver. Remember? Granddad used to call it a damn cabin just to get Cyrus's nose out of joint."

"Everyone called it a cabin except him." Rick's expression was grim as he locked gazes with his brother. "So Cyrus sets up a meeting. Glory goes. She's found dead back in town, and her car is found in town, as well. Why? Why would a woman in her condition go for a walk at night along the river when it was cold and raining? Why would she drive past her house to the park when there's a path to the river right beside her house?"

Anamaria moved her plate to the empty table beside them, unable to face the food any longer. Her stomach was knotted, her skin cold, and just the smell of food made her queasy. Because of the conversation? Because of the baby? Or because she *knew* more had happened that night than a walk.

"Her first appointment that evening was at Lydia's house." Her voice was low but steadier than she'd expected. "Lydia didn't try to keep her meetings with Glory secret from the people close to her. Harrison, Sara and Kent knew about them. Kent spends a lot of time at their house. He was closer to them than to his own parents."

"He could have seen her there that evening." Robbie

clasped her hand in both of his. "He could have been waiting for her and followed her. And when he realized that she was going to meet his father…"

That would have brought out the rage, Anamaria acknowledged. Maybe Glory's death had been accidental, or maybe it had been murder. Either way, one or both of her Calloway lovers had been involved. One of them had taken her baby. Her mother was dead because the passions she'd inspired had been too great, but her sister was alive. True to her name, Charlotte Duquesne had survived.

Abruptly Anamaria pushed back her chair, sprang to her feet and fled the dining room. She bypassed the ladies' room and headed out the door, bumping into guests entering the restaurant, mumbling apologies as she stumbled down the steps. She walked with long steps, not slowing when Robbie called her name, not looking when running steps pounded behind her.

He caught up with her as she started to cross River Road, grabbing her arm, pulling her back as a car sped past, horn blaring. It would be so easy to go into his arms, right there on the main street in town, with people all around, but she didn't…until he pulled her there. He wrapped his arms around her, holding her tightly, and when she tried to point out that people could see, he shushed her.

When the shudders stopped rippling through her, when the sun had warmed the ice from her skin, she raised her head to gaze into his worried blue eyes. "I'm sorry. I just…it just got to be too much."

"She's your mother. Sometimes the rest of us forget that."

"I want to know, but I don't. Maybe I was better off not remembering anything."

He cupped his palm to her cheek, tilting her head back. "You still remembered the night she died. You always remembered the vision you had of her. But you'd blocked out the good memories, too, of baking cookies and walking in the rain and having picnics on that shawl of hers. You'd forgotten about her tucking you in bed, then crawling in beside you to read stories from that book you found in the chest. All of those things are worth remembering, Annie. Those are the kind of memories you treasure for a lifetime."

The kind of memories she intended to make with her own daughter. The kind of memories, God help her, that she wanted Robbie to make with her, too. Fishing out on the river, tramping through the woods, giving her personal tours of the Calloway Plantation. He could teach their daughter what it was like to live in wealth, and Anamaria could remind her what it was like to live in slavery. And she would grow into a wise, understanding young woman—the best of both their worlds.

Rick and Amanda joined them, the latter carrying Anamaria's purse. She handed it over with a hug. "Come to dinner tonight," she murmured. "It'll be good for you."

Rick laid his hand on Robbie's shoulder. "We'll be at Mom's, or I've got my cell if you need anything."

"Thanks, bubba."

Rick and Amanda went back the way they'd come. Robbie kept one arm around Anamaria and hustled her across the road to the car. "Well, Annie," he said, reluctant to let go of her so she could get in. "There's only one person left to talk to."

She swallowed hard and nodded. "Kent."

He nodded, too. "Are you up to it?"

"With you there? You bet." It was mostly bravado, but she would find the courage. She always did.

A phone call to Kent's house confirmed that he was out for the day. "Fishing," Robbie said when he hung up. "That means he's at the cabin. Excuse me, the lodge. How about I take you out to Mom's, and you spend some time getting acquainted with her and Amanda. Then I'll pick you up on my way home."

"You're not going to talk to him without me."

He was worried about her. She still looked pale, still troubled. She'd come to the conclusion back there in the deli that her mother's death might not have been accidental—that even if the fall had been, either Cyrus or Kent, or maybe even both, had done nothing to help her. They had let her die.

She had come to Copper Lake looking for a few details about her mother's last days, and she'd learned more than any daughter would want to know about her last night.

They followed River Road out of town, turning back west onto a narrow dirt road before they reached Calloway Plantation. The road was still muddy from the last rain, and he thought more than once that he should have borrowed Sara's SUV. But they made it through the worst spots and were soon on the uphill slope to the cabin, built atop the riverbank.

Robbie saw no point to a fishing camp when the comforts of home were just a few miles away. Cyrus had seen no point to going home when he could bring the comforts to his camp. The log cabin was built of far more substance than most camps generally were, with a front porch running the length of the building and a back porch on stilts that stretched out over the river for easy fishing. The furniture inside was made of leather and wood, the rugs Navajo, the art fairly good. When Robbie was young, it had been used for entertaining out-of-town business associates, but most of the family had preferred to do their fishing from a boat or sitting on a quiet bank somewhere.

A black Escalade was parked in front of the cabin. Robbie pulled in next to it, got out and circled the car to help

Anamaria out. The scene was quiet—no television or music from inside, no rocking or conversation on the front porch.

They climbed the steps to the porch and he rang the doorbell, listening to it echo inside. Before it faded away, a board creaked to his left and Kent stepped around the corner.

"What do you want?"

Kent's welcomes were never very welcoming. He disliked everyone to some extent, and he disliked Robbie and his brothers more. Maybe it was because they'd had a lousy father, too, but they hadn't let it hold them back. Maybe because their mother *wasn't* lousy. Sara had devoted herself to raising her kids, while Mary had just abandoned hers.

"Anamaria and I wanted to talk to you."

Kent came a few steps closer, then eased one hip onto the porch railing. "I figured you'd come along eventually, if you were smart enough to figure it out."

"We've figured out a few things."

"Like what?"

Robbie faced Kent fully. "That Glory was your father's mistress. That she was sleeping with you, too. That Cyrus got her pregnant."

Kent bitterly shook his head. "Now, I missed that. I never knew about him and her until that night. I thought the baby was mine. The timing was right. She told me I was the only one she'd been with. Lying whore. Even when she broke up with me a few weeks before the baby was due, even when she said then that the baby wasn't mine, I didn't believe her. All I wanted was to marry her and stop sneaking around and live like normal people, her and me and our baby. Just be a real family."

"She had another baby," Robbie pointed out, gesturing toward Anamaria. "What about her?"

Kent's gaze flickered over her derisively. "She had family to take her in. She didn't need to be with us."

It sounded callous—it *was* callous. But given Glory's history, who could blame Kent for thinking she would agree? She'd given away custody of her first two daughters; why not the third?

"But Glory turned you down," Robbie prompted.

"No, she didn't," Kent hastily responded. "She said she needed some time. Said she needed to get herself together for the baby's birth, and then we'd talk.

"I kept waiting for her to call, but she never did. Every day, every night. Then that night I was on my way over to Aunt Lydia's and I saw her leaving. It was raining real hard, and that car of hers was always giving her trouble, so I decided to follow her home, just to make sure she got there. Only she didn't go home."

The downpour would have made it cold and miserable, Anamaria thought, and would have turned the road to the cabin into soupy mud. In her mind, she could see Glory in her little secondhand car—*It may be a junker, but God love her, she's my junker*—trying to navigate the road. Cyrus waited at this end in his fancy fishing cabin, with more money than he knew what to do with and a baby or grandbaby about to make an appearance in the world. She could have turned around at any point and gone home, but she'd forged ahead for Charlotte's sake, for her family's sake.

"When she saw my headlights behind her, she thought I was my father," Kent said, his voice flat and distant. "She pulled over, hoping to avoid the rest of the drive up here. She about jumped out of her skin when she saw it was me at her window. She told me to go home, told me I was going to ruin everything. I didn't know what she was talking about. God, I was a damn fool.

"That was when she told me, standing in the rain down there on the road, freezing our asses off. She'd been sleeping with my father longer than she'd known me. This kid that I was willing to marry her for, to give up everything for, was his snot-nosed bastard. My own freakin' half sister."

Anamaria walked to the top of the steps, facing out, the scene playing out in her mind as his words continued. He'd howled like a wounded animal when Glory had told him Cyrus was Charlotte's father, and he'd slapped her, knocking her to the ground. Immediately apologetic, he'd offered his hand, but instead she'd kicked out at him, hitting him squarely in the testicles. As he'd sunk to the ground with another howl of pain, she'd pushed to her feet and started running. Her shawl was all she had to keep her dry, and it wasn't made for that. It slipped and tree branches snagged at it, but she clenched the ends tightly in her hands and ran on, heart pounding, abdomen cramping, angling through the woods for the river.

Kent had lain there in the mud, sniveling, trying twice to get to his feet before managing to do so. Soaked to the skin, in pain, sucking air in small gasps, he'd taken a few halting steps after her. Every movement throbbed, fueling his disillusionment and betrayal, until rage overcame pain. He'd caught her on the path, roaring her name. She'd looked over her shoulder, crying loudly enough for him to hear over the rain, and then she'd turned back and fallen.

"You didn't go for help," Robbie said quietly, his voice jarring Anamaria from the scene. Hugging herself tightly, she turned to look at them: Kent, once a twenty-year-old boy, in love and determined to be a better father than his father could have ever been…only to find out that Cyrus had been Glory's lover first. Had fathered the child Kent believed was his own.

And Robbie…somber, strong, capable, concerned for her. *I'm the shallow one, the superficial one, the irresponsible one,* he'd said, but it was so much bull. Maybe when he was a boy,

but boys were allowed those faults. He was a man to be proud
of. A man who would do what was right.

Kent's voice was barely audible. "She was hurt bad. Her
head was all gashed open, and she was having trouble breathing and seeing things that weren't there. I couldn't have
carried her back, and if I'd left to get someone, it would have
been too late. The baby was already coming, and Glory was
already going."

She wasn't seeing things that weren't there. It was
Grandma Chessie, Moon, Florence and plenty of the others
who'd gone on before. They'd been waiting to welcome her.
Birthing was the hard part, coming into the world all alone.
Passing to meet again with people you loved, who loved you
back, was sweet and easy.

Tears moistened Anamaria's cheeks as she spoke for the
first time. "You were there when our sister was born."

Kent stared at her as if he'd never seen her before, then
swallowed hard, making the connection. His father, her
mother. "She came sliding out into the water. I wrapped her
in Glory's shawl. I was going to leave her there, but…"

It was likely true that he couldn't help Glory, but the baby
was another matter. If he took her, she would live; if he left
her, she would die. Anamaria couldn't help but think Cyrus
would have made a different decision.

"Where did you take her?"

"Someplace safe."

"Where?" Robbie asked.

But Kent's eyes darkened, his jaw clamped shut and he
folded his arms over his chest for emphasis.

A long moment passed, birds singing, sun shining, a boat
putting by on the river. A perfectly normal day. And all
Anamaria wanted to do was grieve in Robbie's arms.

Robbie finally broke the silence. He moved closer to Kent,

laying his hand on his shoulder, the way Rick had done with him a short time earlier. "Will you go into town with us and talk to Tommy?"

Kent turned away, staring out over the woods through which Glory had fled to her death, and his sigh seemed to well up from the depths of his soul. "Why not? What's left to lose? Let me lock up the cabin."

The screen door bumped shut behind him. Robbie joined Anamaria at the steps, wrapping his arms around her from behind. "You were right. Charlotte survived."

She smiled thinly. "Yeah. I wonder how many tens of thousands of mixed-race twenty-three-year-old girls I'll have to go through to find her. Because, you know, Mama Odette won't be able to die in peace without seeing her grandbaby."

"That should keep her around another twenty years at least. Maybe she'll give Chessie a run for the money in the age department."

Anamaria was thinking about the small pleasure that Robbie remembered the many names and details of the Duquesne family she'd thrown out over the past few days, and about the bigger pleasure when he would get to meet them— the living ones, at least—hopefully soon. They would be so happy to find out that she was in love and pregnant, and they would be shocked to hear that she'd decided curses were for lesser women than Duquesnes. If Robbie was willing to take a chance on her, the least she could do was take the same chance on him. For their baby's sake. For their sake.

And who knew? Maybe Kent would relent before then and tell them where he'd taken Charlotte. Maybe the sister everyone had thought dead could be at her wedding to the man she would live the rest of her life with.

Then a gunshot rang out.

* * *

Robbie and Anamaria sat on the porch steps, Rick on one side, Tommy on the other. The sheriff and his deputies were inside the cabin, along with the medical examiner's staff. Suicide, they all agreed. No one could have known. No one could have prevented it.

Robbie wasn't so sure.

As if he'd read his mind, Rick slid his arm around Robbie's shoulders, mussed his hair, then pulled his head to his own shoulder. "It's not your fault, bubba. People are gonna do what they're gonna do. Kent's never been happy a day in his life, except maybe those months with Glory. He wasn't making a plea for help. It wasn't a gesture. He wanted it done."

A single bullet to the brain had certainly gotten it done. "Still...I shouldn't have let him go into the cabin alone. I should have known he wouldn't have come out here without a gun. Granddad taught us better than that."

"Granddad taught us a lot," Rick said. "Some of it didn't take with Kent."

"He's right, Rob," Tommy said. "Kent's been miserable the last twenty-three years. Maybe now he can find some peace." He glanced over his shoulder, then stood up and offered his hand to Anamaria. "They're ready to bring his body out. Why don't you two go on?"

Robbie didn't look over his shoulder, didn't want to see into the living room with its leather furniture and Navajo rugs, stained now with blood, didn't want to see the zippered bag that contained Kent's body. He hadn't cared much for Kent, but, God, he hadn't wanted this.

The four of them walked to the Vette in silence, and he and Anamaria headed back toward town in the same, heavy silence. She kept her hand on his thigh, her touch reassuring.

He could live with that touch for the next sixty years and never grow tired of its comfort, its familiarity.

If she would have him.

As he turned onto the highway, she asked, "Where would he have gone that night, Robbie? He was twenty years old, he had a newborn child in need of food, clothing and attention, and he had a car to move to make sure that no one connected Glory's last night with his family. Where would he have taken Charlotte? Who could he have trusted with her?"

The answer was simple, sure. "Lydia." She had loved Kent like a son. She would have accepted whatever story he told her and would have taken his secret to her grave.

Lydia. Glory's friend. But blood was thicker than water.

He drove through town, then turned east on Carolina. They passed the mall, the turn that led to Marguerite and the nursing home, the elaborate brick-and-iron gates that led to Cyrus's property and finally reached Twin Oaks. Lydia was sitting in a rocker on the broad porch, her head bowed over a small bundle in her arms.

"She knows," Anamaria murmured.

"Yeah." He didn't have to be a psychic to see.

Robbie parked next to her car, then took Anamaria's hand as they crossed the drive to the steps. Lydia didn't look up but continued her slow, steady rocking. "Glory used to say that when we die, the people who loved us are waiting to meet us. I like that idea, seeing all those people who have already passed on. But who do you suppose was there to meet Kent?"

Anamaria pulled free of Robbie and crouched in front of the rocker. "Mr. John was there, and another man—tall, slender, with big hands and big ears."

Robbie stiffened, but Lydia smiled even though her eyes were damp. "That's his granddad Jed. Jed's mama used to say that God gave him those ears so she'd have something to hold on to when she had to wallop him for misbehaving."

Anamaria had seen his granddad at the cabin. The news knocked Robbie back on his heels. He hadn't noticed—she hadn't said... But in eight words, she'd given a perfect description of a man she'd never seen. And if he believed in spirits and crossing over, Granddad was the one person who would always be there to welcome his grandchildren. Even when they'd exasperated or disappointed him, he'd still loved them. Always loved them.

"Miss Lydia, Kent told us he took the baby. He wrapped her in Mama's shawl, and he took her someplace safe." Anamaria's voice was soft and unsteady, and so was her hand as she touched the bundle Lydia cradled. "He brought her to you, didn't he?"

It was the shawl she held, Robbie realized. Duquesne family history, taken from Glory as she lay dying, and Lydia had had it all these years.

Before Lydia could answer, the front door slammed open with a bang and Harrison Kennedy strode out. "What the hell are you doing here? I told you you couldn't talk to her! I forbade you—"

"Harrison," Lydia interrupted. "For heaven's sake, it's Robbie. He's family. Of course he can talk to me. I was just about to tell them about the baby. About Charlotte."

Harrison stabbed a finger in her direction. "You don't tell them anything. We agreed never to discuss it, remember?"

She made a dismissive gesture. "That was years ago, and Kent's gone now, bless his heart. He doesn't need our protection anymore."

Harrison mimicked the same gesture. "It was never about protecting him, Liddy! Maybe if he'd had to face the consequences of his actions, it would have turned him into a man.

But he couldn't have paid without dragging you into it, and I never would have let that happen. I *won't* let that happen." Abruptly, he stabbed his finger at Robbie. "You're still our damn lawyer. Anything she says to you is privileged. You can't tell a soul."

"That was why you insisted I handle this myself, wasn't it?" Robbie asked. "You didn't want a private investigator because privilege wouldn't apply. If he found evidence of a crime, he would have to report it, but I couldn't."

Lydia shooed Anamaria back, then got to her feet to face her husband. "Harrison, just what crime do you think I committed?"

"That woman…the baby…" He dragged his fingers through his hair. "She was here that night—came to swindle Liddy out of more money. I left to have dinner at the country club and play a few hands of poker. When I came home, Kent was tearing up the driveway like a bat out of hell, the woman was gone and Liddy was sitting in the parlor holding that damn baby, cooing, going on like it was her own."

"You thought I—" Lydia blanched, and her mouth worked a moment before she started again. "You thought I—I did something to Glory to get her baby? You thought I *killed* her?"

Harrison's face turned as red as hers was pale. "She was alive and well and pregnant when I left, and when I come back, there's no sign of her but the baby? And the next morning she's found dead by the river on the other side of town? What was I supposed to think?"

"Mr. Kennedy, my mother died where her body was found," Anamaria said quietly. "She and Kent were arguing. She ran into the woods to get away from him, and she fell. He left her there, but he brought the baby to Miss Lydia."

Now it was his turn to gape, his jaw working.

"Harrison, how could you think for a second that I would harm Glory?" Lydia asked sorrowfully.

His gaze flickered around the group before settling on her. "You wanted a baby so bad. You were never the same after ours— The way you looked at pregnant women, the way you looked at babies... There was such heartache. And you wouldn't tell me anything. All you did was stare at that baby like your world was right again."

"So you didn't call the police because you were afraid of what Lydia had done," Robbie said. "And the next morning, when you heard that Glory was dead..."

Harrison took a step back, leaning against the wall as if he badly needed the support. "I called Doc Josephs. He took the baby, and I took Liddy to New York, to see a doctor friend of his there. Josephs arranged through another doctor for some people to take the baby. My lawyer took care of the details."

"Your lawyer," Robbie repeated. "Uncle Cyrus. Charlotte's father." The coldhearted bastard had helped with the adoption of his own child and, knowing him, collected a large sum of money for it. Had he cared about Glory's death? Had he considered claiming his daughter for even a moment?

Lucky for Charlotte, apparently not. She'd had a chance to grow up in a normal home, to be happy and well-adjusted and well-loved. Her first hours of life had hopefully been the toughest of her life.

He moved to take Anamaria's hand, lacing his fingers tightly through hers. He wanted to walk away with her, to take her home and make love to her, hold her, comfort her. He wanted to drive to Savannah with her, to meet Mama Odette and Aunties Charise and Lueena and give them the news about Charlotte in person.

He wanted to tell her he loved her. To ask her to marry him.

He wanted to tell her he believed—in her gifts, in her, in them, in forever.

"What happens now?" Harrison asked, subdued for the first time in all the years Robbie had known him.

Robbie gazed at Anamaria. There was sorrow in her eyes but also hope and peace, and that serenity that made her so damn beautiful. After a moment, he looked back at Harrison and Lydia. "Kent's already paid for his part. We tell Tommy the rest and let the authorities decide." Then he winked at Anamaria. "And we find Charlotte. Tommy will be in touch."

He and Anamaria had reached the bottom of the steps when he let go and went back, pulling the shawl from Lydia's hands. She was gazing at Harrison, her hold limp, and didn't notice the fabric slipping away. Back at the steps, he shook out the folds, then, despite the sun's warmth, wrapped the faded wools and velvets around Anamaria's slender shoulders.

Knotting his fingers in the fabric on either side, he gazed down at her, so incredibly beautiful, so amazingly important. To think that a week ago, he hadn't known she existed, that only a few days ago he'd thought the difficulties of a relationship with her too much to overcome. How had everything changed so completely, so quickly?

He'd never been one to question good fortune. Why start now?

"Don't go back to Savannah, Annie. Stay with me. Live with me. Marry me."

Her smile was slight, impossible to read.

"I know we haven't known each other very long—"

She raised her fingers to his mouth. "It's not how long that matters. It's how well. Destiny doesn't count time like we do."

After kissing her fingers, he brushed them away. "Am I your destiny?"

This time her smile was bright and happy…and reminded him of the photograph of her and Glory in front of their church. Destined to steal a man's breath, he'd thought when he'd first seen it. Along with his heart. "Oh, yes, chile, and I'm yours." She pointed her finger at him, nearly tapping his nose. "And don't you go trying to forget it. You. Me. Our daughters. Meant to be."

He let go of the shawl ends, and she raised her arms to enclose him in it, too. *Meant to be.* Damn, but he liked the sound of that. And *daughters.* He liked the sound of that, too. Nuzzling her neck, he murmured, "Let's go home, Annie, and start working on those daughters."

With a laugh, she pulled away and twirled in a circle, the shawl flowing around her. "We've already done that, darlin'. But I'm happy to practice for the second one."

He didn't ask how she could know so soon. She was a Duquesne woman, and Duquesne women knew things. And she was his woman, though he knew only one thing: He loved her. Wanted her. Needed her.

Forever.

It was a cold, rainy January evening, but there was a party going on in Labor and Delivery at Copper Lake Medical Center. Room 312 was filled with people, with soft voices and laughter and the scent of incredible food brought in from the deli. Anamaria sat in bed, the top raised so she could lean against it, and gazed at the baby in her arms. Less than twelve hours old, perfect in every way, with cocoa-hued skin and Calloway blue eyes, seven pounds, seven ounces and nineteen inches long. The baby scent was so sweet, and so were the miniature gown and the tiny little hands that flailed in the air.

She'd never known instant love—she almost had with Robbie. But she'd loved this child from the moment she'd known of its existence, and now, able to stroke the soft baby skin, to smooth the fine hair, to nestle her cheek against her child's, she was overwhelmed by love. For the baby. For Robbie. For all the family, Duquesnes and Calloways alike, who had joined them.

Her husband sat beside her, looking as tired as if *he'd* spent fifteen hours in labor. Technically, he had, but she'd done all the work.

"Have you decided on a name yet?" Mama Odette asked from the chair closest to the bed.

Anamaria smiled. She had. She'd decided on Gloriane the moment she'd known she was pregnant. But the baby—and destiny—had thrown a wrench in *that* plan. "We have," she replied. "Robert William Calloway Jr. And we'll call him Will."

"Hey, Will," his daddy said, letting the tiny fingers clench around his own finger. "Welcome to our world."

Yes, she, Anamaria Duquesne Calloway, had broken the two-hundred-year-old curse. First she'd gotten married, and now her pretty little baby girl had turned out to be a beautiful little baby boy.

The Duquesne curse had turned into a blessing.

And she'd never been happier.

* * * * *

Harlequin is 60 years old,
and Harlequin Blaze is celebrating!
After all, a lot can happen in 60 years,
or 60 minutes...or 60 seconds!

Find out what's going down in
Blaze's heart-stopping new miniseries,
FROM 0 TO 60!
Getting from "Hello" to "How was it?"
can happen fast....

Here's a sneak peek of the first book,

A LONG, HARD RIDE
by Alison Kent

Available March 2009

"IS THAT FOR ME?" Trey asked.

Cardin Worth cocked her head to the side and considered how much better the day already seemed. "Good morning to you, too."

When she didn't hold out the second cup of coffee for him to take, he came closer. She sipped from her heavy white mug, hiding her grin and her giddy rush of nerves behind it.

But when he stopped in front of her, she made the mistake of lowering her gaze from his face to the exposed strip of his chest. It was either give him his cup of coffee or bury her nose against him and breathe in. She remembered so clearly how he smelled. How he tasted.

She gave him his coffee.

After taking a quick gulp, he smiled and said, "Good morning, Cardin. I hope the floor wasn't too hard for you."

The hardness of the floor hadn't been the problem. She

shook her head. "Are you kidding? I slept like a baby, swaddled in my sleeping bag."

"In my sleeping bag, you mean."

If he wanted to get technical, yeah. "Thanks for the loaner. It made sleeping on the floor almost bearable." As had the warmth of his spooned body, she thought, then quickly changed the subject. "I saw you have a loaf of bread and some eggs. Would you like me to cook breakfast?"

He lowered his coffee mug slowly, his gaze as warm as the sun on her shoulders, as the ceramic heating her hands. "I didn't bring you out here to wait on me."

"You didn't bring me out here at all. I volunteered to come."

"To help me get ready for the race. Not to serve me."

"It's just breakfast, Trey. And coffee." Even if last night it had been more. Even if the way he was looking at her made her want to climb back into that sleeping bag. "I work much better when my stomach's not growling. I thought it might be the same for you."

"It is, but I'll cook. You made the coffee."

"That's because I can't work at all without caffeine."

"If I'd known that, I would've put on a pot as soon I got up."

"What time *did* you get up?" Judging by the sun's position, she swore it couldn't be any later than seven now. And, yeah, they'd agreed to start working at six.

"Maybe four?" he guessed, giving her a lazy smile.

"But it was almost two..." She let the sentence dangle, finishing the thought privately. She was quite sure he knew exactly what time they'd finally fallen asleep after he'd made love to her.

The question facing her now was where did this relationship—if you could even call it *that*—go from here?

* * * * *

*Cardin and Trey are about to find out that
great sex is only the beginning….
Don't miss the fireworks!
Get ready for*

*A LONG, HARD RIDE
by Alison Kent*

*Available March 2009,
wherever Blaze books are sold.*

CELEBRATE
60 YEARS
OF PURE READING PLEASURE
WITH HARLEQUIN®!

**We'll be spotlighting a different series
every month throughout 2009
to celebrate our 60th anniversary.**

Look for Harlequin® Blaze™ in March!

O-60

*After all, a lot can happen in 60 years,
or 60 minutes...or 60 seconds!*

Find out what's going down in Blaze's
heart-stopping new miniseries *0-60!*
Getting from "Hello" to "How was it?"
can happen fast....

Look for the brand-new 0-60 miniseries in March 2009!

REQUEST YOUR FREE BOOKS!

2 FREE NOVELS PLUS 2 FREE GIFTS!

Silhouette® Romantic

SUSPENSE

Sparked by Danger, Fueled by Passion!

SRS08R

HARLEQUIN® Romance®

This February the Harlequin® Romance series
will feature six Diamond Brides stories featuring
diamond proposals and gorgeous grooms.

Share your dream wedding proposal and you could WIN!

The most romantic entry will win a diamond
necklace and will inspire a proposal in one of
our upcoming Diamond Grooms books in 2010.

In 100 words or less, tell us the most romantic
way that you dream of being proposed to.

For more information, and to enter
the Diamond Brides Proposal contest, please visit
www.DiamondBridesProposal.com

Or mail your entry to us at:
IN THE U.S.: 3010 Walden Ave., P.O. Box 9069, Buffalo, NY 14269-9069
IN CANADA: 225 Duncan Mill Road, Don Mills, ON M3B 3K9

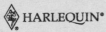

INTRIGUE

SPECIAL OPS
TEXAS
COWBOY COMMANDO

BY JOANNA WAYNE

When Linney Kingston's best friend dies in
a drowning accident one day after she told
Linney she was leaving her abusive husband,
Linney is convinced the husband killed her. Linney
goes to the one man she knows can help her, an
ex lover who she's never been able to forget—
Navy SEAL Cutter Martin. They will have to
work together to solve the mystery, but can
they leave their past behind them?

Available March 2009 wherever you buy books.

Romantic

SUSPENSE

COMING NEXT MONTH

Available February 24, 2009

#1551 THE RANCHER BODYGUARD—Carla Cassidy
Wild West Bodyguards
Grace Covington's stepfather has been murdered, her teenage sister the only suspect. Convinced of her sister's innocence, Grace turns to her ex-boyfriend, attorney Charlie Black, to help her find the truth. Although she's determined not to forgive his betrayal, the sexual tension instantly returns as their investigation leads them into danger…and back into each other's arms.

#1552 CLAIMED BY THE SECRET AGENT—Lyn Stone
Special Ops
COMPASS agent Grant Tyndal was supposed to be on a mission to rescue a kidnapping victim, but Marie Beauclair doesn't need rescuing. An undercover CIA operative, she's perfectly able to save herself. As they work together to catch the kidnapper, will the high-intensity situations turn their high-voltage passion into something more?

#1553 SAFE BY HIS SIDE—Linda Conrad
The Safekeepers
When someone begins stalking a child star, Ethan Ryan is the perfect man to be her bodyguard. But the child's guardian, Blythe Cooper, wants nothing to do with him. As the stalker closes in, sparks fly between Ethan and Blythe, and they soon find their lives—and their hearts—at risk.

#1554 SUSPECT LOVER—Stephanie Doyle
They both wanted a family, so Caroline Sommerville and Dominic Santos agreed to a marriage of convenience. Neither expected love—until it happened. But when Dominic's business partner is murdered, he's the prime suspect and goes on the run. Can Caroline trust this man who lied about his past—the man she now calls her husband?

SRSCNMBPA0209